Dare to Dream

Pam Hilliard

A catalogue record for this book is available from the National Library of Australia

Linellen Press
265 Boomerang Road
Oldbury, Western Australia
www.linellenpress.com.au

Dedication

This book is dedicated to my amazing family, Bruce, Michael, and Daniel for supporting me through all of my crazy equestrian pursuits and believing in my ability to conquer new ventures.

Contents

Chapter 1

Good Morning

Squinting as her eyes opened to the brilliant sunlight bearing down on her through her open window, Aimee stirred slowly from her sleep, and her dream. She turned her head from the glare, let her gaze drift over the endless pictures of her favourite equestrian heroes who inspired her every day, their achievements spurring her on to her goal. They had done it, *so anything is possible, right?*

Her dream faded with her awakening: she was no longer sitting astride a magnificent black horse, saluting the judge; no longer dressed in immaculate top hat and tails, spotless white breeches and shiny black boots. The centre line of the arena was now her bed, and she was dressed in her crumpled mauve pyjamas. *One day*, she thought positively, turning over. *One day I will be a champion dressage rider; one day I will teach others just like me. One day …*

She buried her head in her pillow. *One day … One day …*

… if only Mum would share my dreams, or even understand them.

She buried her head deeper, avoiding the thought of rising, and wondered what state her mother would be in this morning; wondered what she would need to do for her before she headed off to school. The thought jabbed at her and prodded her to rise — something she couldn't put off because it was always there waiting for her, no matter how long it took for her to face it. And routine was the only way to cope with it.

Turning over again, Aimee swung her legs out of bed and stood, ready to start the routine. First off: say good morning to her vast array of riders on the wall, as she had done each day for the past three years. Then it was into morning chores: make the bed, tidy her desk and pack her homework into her bag ready for school. Then make breakfast, and her lunch so she'd be ready for school.

Then it was time to check on her mum – mainly to check that she was still breathing. So far, she always had been, which meant she needed to sort out her needs – a cup of coffee and toast on her bedside cabinet; pull back the curtains and throw light into the house; pick up the empty bottles and dump them in the trash; take some money from her purse, if there was any, to buy food for dinner on her way home. With this routine, she would have it all done by the time the bus appeared at the corner, and she was ready to endure the adventures at school. With this routine, she would make sure the teachers at Wandeering High School remained unaware of her situation. As long as she showed no signs of neglect, they wouldn't suspect anything was wrong … different … She just had to keep going like this until she gained the lifestyle she wished for … when she became famous.

Swinging her backpack over her shoulder, she headed for the bus.

Fridays always dragged on; the usual classes never really interested her. The only good thing about Fridays was it was nearly Saturday, and Saturday was her riding day. Saturday was her day of work and pleasure.

Two years ago, when she was twelve, she had scored a job at Trailblazers Riding School, which was close enough to ride her bike to, which meant she could work for her lessons and not have to rely on anyone to help her.

Her passion for riding horses had started as a toddler sitting on the merry-go-round horses at the Royal Show. In later years, she had watched competitors in the arena competing for the colourful ribbons.

Then fate stepped in, and after taking a wrong turn on her bike through the back areas of a nearby suburb, the Trailblazers sign with the picture of a smiling Sarah Brown, Head Instructor, reinforced the fire for her to ride. Sarah's smiling face almost spoke to her – 'You can do this!' She had researched Sarah Brown, out of curiosity, and found magazine articles written about her successful dressage career, a career that had ended abruptly.

It had only been a matter of time, and a few more rides past that sign before she had pedalled up that driveway, responding to a HELP WANTED ad on the sign, her heart pounding with extreme possibilities. She was now fourteen, and Sarah called her 'my right arm'.

Saturday came, and Aimee prayed as she whisked through her morning routine that nothing would prevent her from leaving on time. She made her bed, scoffed down breakfast while she prepared her mother's and headed out to her bike. This was always the best day of the week. This was the day she had an adventure, and always came home with a sense of achievement. She felt the calmness flow over her as she pedalled down the road.

While she was a little conscious of her height, being taller than most girls her age, her long slender legs helped speed her along on the fifteen-minute journey, so much so her long black ponytail swung out behind her. She smiled to herself – Sarah had said her long slim legs and slender frame made her the perfect shape for a dressage rider. She could drape her legs around the horse's side without having to stretch to look elegant, and she could mount even the taller horses, like Monnie, without a mounting block. And while her skin tone was a lot fairer than Sarah's, she noticed it darkening a little with the longer hours she worked outside in the sun.

As she rode down the hill, Trailblazers appeared before her, the prominent indoor arena standing out amongst the tall trees of the entrance way. From the top of the hill, the forty acres of lush green paddocks spread out, dotted with an array of thoroughly contented horses. Aimee approached the entrance, her dark eyes sweeping over the colourful Trailblazer sign with its images of dressage horses and perfectly aligned riders, and showjumpers, denoting what was taught within the training centre. In particular, she loved the image of Sarah Brown in the circle in the bottom right corner, and Karen Heizmen, her head stablehand in the bottom left corner. Both women were smiling, showing it was a friendly place to learn. She pedalled on up the driveway.

"Good morning, my star pupil. How are we today?" greeted her as she swung into the stable yard and propped her bike against the back of a shed, out of harm's way.

"Wonderful," Aimee replied with a smile. "Do we have lots on today, Sarah?"

"Heaps," Sarah laughed. "Six lessons today, starting at eight. I need you to get Floppy, Rinso and Barney ready for me and make up the lunchtime feeds. Can you do that?"

Aimee nodded. "Of course. I'm onto it."

This was the best job ever: it paid for her lessons, and she loved working with the horses. Any job she was given was a joy and often a learning experience and how she loved learning from Sarah. She was the absolute best, and Aimee dreamt of being a top riding coach and dressage champion just like her. She even had the same dark eyes and long dark hair, which she wore up in a ponytail, and which Aimee copied. So she was off to a good, emulating start.

"Oh … and would you like to ride Monnie in the eleven o'clock lesson. I need a star pupil to demonstrate riding accurate circles?" Sarah asked.

"Ride Monnie? Oh, would I!" shouted Aimee. "Thank you!"

As if Sarah didn't know she would be thrilled to ride Sarah's best horse. Of all the horses at Trailblazers, Monnie was the best and Aimee was thrilled that, for the last year, she was the only one who rode her.

On that note, she promptly disappeared into the tack room to carry out her tasks of lugging out saddles, bridles and saddle rugs, and checking all were in good order. Then she gathered up grooming kits for each horse and set them ready at the tie-up post. Next, she brought out Floppy, Rinso and Barney, brushed them down and saddled them ready, the bridles left hanging on their hooks until the riders were ready. The work was strenuous but Aimee loved it, and she could manage lifting a saddle onto a pony's back with only a little stretching.

When the ponies were bridled and taken away for their lesson, Aimee mixed the feeds for the horse's lunches, measuring the right amount of grains for each horse according to their feed chart on the whiteboard – yet which she knew off by heart. When that was done, she looked for other tasks – swept the corridor, then checked the tack room was in order. By then it was only 9.30 am. *Only an hour and a half till my lesson*, she sighed. To pass the time, she placed all the feeds into the feed bins, ready for the hungry horses to return.

The time drew nearer, and Aimee prepared for her lesson by fetching Monnie's headstall and lead rope, and making her way down to the bottom paddock where Monnie grazed, the black mare totally oblivious to her arrival. Monnie's stomach was always more important to her, and Aimee always came armed with a handful of carrots and an apple, knowing this would make catching her easier.

After securing the headstall on Monnie's head and attaching the lead rope, she began feeding Monnie the bribes. "I'm going to ride you today, so I hope you behave yourself for me," Aimee said as she started making her way back to the stables. She'd performed this task many times without any incidents and felt relaxed as Monnie ambled calmly at her shoulder. But this time, in a split second, Monnie propped, swung her head up and around and shot backwards, reefing Aimee almost off her feet.

Aimee squealed. "What's up, Monnie? … what is it, girl?" She tried to soothe the mare once she'd regained her footing on the loose stones, her own nerves rattled. It was so unlike Monnie. Shooting a glance over her shoulder; she spotted a big, brown snake slithering away from the path.

"Wow. Thanks, Monnie," Aimee said, heaving a sigh of relief. The snake had been so close. She patted Monnie's neck reassuringly and slipped her another carrot. "That would have put a dampener on the day." She shook her head. "That's the fourth one this year," and she chastised herself for not keeping a more watchful eye for them, especially on hot days like this – it was always the unseen ones that posed the biggest problems.

Taking a couple of deep breaths and allowing the snake time to get well away, she headed back to the stables to tell Sarah about the snake, Monnie ambling gallantly at her side. "You saved me that time, you beautiful girl," she said, stroking the mare's glossy black neck again. "You're my protector, so keep watching."

Back at the stables, after she'd told Sarah about what had happened, and everyone had been warned to keep alert to the snake's presence, it was all go. Sarah assigned horses to pupils for the 10.30 lesson, which Karen, her head girl, would teach. The young woman had been with Sarah for two years and had many years' teaching experience. Aimee had learnt a lot from watching her teach as well. As Sarah allocated the appropriate horses and ponies to pupils, Karen conducted the compulsory safety checks before the lesson, ensuring the horse or pony was not injured in any way, and that the gear fitted correctly. Then she adjusted the girths to prevent the saddles from slipping. This also checked the rider's ability to tack up their own horse for the lesson and their proficiency in stable management, which was an important component of horse ownership.

As Karen assembled her Level Four students outside the arena ready for the class to begin, Sarah walked into the arena to set up the cavallettis and aids for the canter work Karen would take the class through.

"You'd better start getting Monnie ready, sweetie," she told Aimee, reminding her of the nearness of time.

Aimee's heart leapt. *Yes, it's time.* The very best part of her week. Swiftly, but thoroughly, she brushed Monnie's coat with the body brush, combed her pulled mane, then picked out her hooves to clear them of foreign matter. All the time, as Sarah had taught her, she kept her hands moving over the mare as a way of checking Monnie's general health, stimulating her muscles and relaxing Monnie for the lesson. Then she fastened the shin boots onto each leg to protect Monnie if she knocked herself, ensuring the boot tags all faced to the back so they wouldn't catch on anything and slip down. Having checked they were secure and not too tight, Aimee fetched the gear, feeling privileged to be using Sarah's good KN dressage saddle, and not just one of the ordinary school saddles.

Placing the saddle blanket on Monnie's back, she made sure it sat equally over the withers, then placed the saddle on Monnie's back and slid it and the blanket back till it sat in the correct position. Then she pulled the front of the saddle blanket up into the pommel to prevent any rubbing, which would make Monnie sore – she would hate for Monnie to suffer for her carelessness, and would be so ashamed if Sarah realised she hadn't saddled her correctly. Next, she secured the girth, ensuring she could fit two fingers between the horse's side and the girth. She then put Monnie's bridle on by placing the bridle's headpiece at the top of Monnie's head and guiding the bit into her mouth, using her left fingers to open it. Her right hand then guided the bridle up into position and eased the headpiece over Monnie's ears so it sat evenly over her poll. With the throat lash buckled up to keep the bridle on and the noseband Monnie wore to keep her mouth shut so she couldn't lean on the bit, Aimee was ready to climb on board for her lesson.

As she entered the indoor arena, she noticed she shared it with two other pupils, both outsiders with their own ponies. The riders appeared to be her age, but clearly were more experienced. This made Aimee more determined to accomplish any task Sarah asked of her.

Sarah stood in the middle of the arena and confidentially started the lesson. "Good morning, everyone. Today, we are going to practice straight lines, circles and simple changes. It all sounds simple enough but trying to ride them accurately for a dressage test is harder that one thinks.

"Form up in single file behind Simone, five horses' distance apart," Sarah instructed, getting straight into the lesson. "Simone, at a walk, turn down the centre line at A. Keep as straight as you can and don't take your eyes off C. See how straight your line is."

The three girls soon realised the difficulties in actually riding a straight line without wavering. Sarah then placed two poles in the centre of the arena, creating a track for the girls to ride between. Even though this assisted them with the direction, the girls soon realised how vital it was to sit equally balanced on the seatbones to ride a perfect line.

The lesson continued and, to Aimee, the concepts of accuracy became clearer with each exercise. At the conclusion of the lesson, she felt confident she would not only be able to begin her dressage career at Preliminary level, but also felt confident enough to do it in open competition. The only problem with achieving this was that she didn't have the equipment – not a horse, a saddle or any of the riding attire essential for any competition and, as her mother had never been in a fit state to ever watch her ride, she knew she was not likely to ever get the support or equipment she needed. Though constantly disappointed by this, she never gave up on her dreams.

With the lesson finished, Aimee returned to the stables, unsaddled Monnie, hosed all the sweat off her and then put her out in the paddock, the mare soon finding a nice sandy spot for an energetic roll. Then Aimee continued with the new chores allocated to her until she heard Sarah calling: "Come on, Aimee, I'm starving. Let's go up for lunch.

"That was a great lesson today," she continued as Aimee fell into step beside her as they headed for the house. "You rode Monnie very well."

"I really felt I learnt a lot today. Thank you. I would love to practice some simple changes again at a later stage … if you don't mind."

"How about tomorrow? Are you able to ride her again tomorrow?" Sarah asked.

"Oh yes, please, Sarah! That would be fantastic!" Aimee almost squealed the words out, and a beaming smile spread across her face. More quietly, she hoped she would have as much fun as she'd had that day.

As the afternoon moved on, Aimee finished all of her chores and, saying goodbye to Sarah and Karen, retrieved her bike and headed for home, reminiscing about the lesson and how much closer she felt to achieving her goal. Eventually, she wondered what new dilemmas her mother might have created for her.

Chapter 2

Unwelcomed Surprise

As Aimee rode up the short red driveway, she stopped pedalling. The front door stood wide open – her mother wouldn't leave it like that. *So what's going on?*

Placing her bike in the garage, she walked cautiously through the front door, not knowing what to expect. Clothes were strewn everywhere. Dishes were in the sink. It all appeared normal, and she breathed a sigh of relief – her mother must have left the front door open by accident. Then she noticed the silence.

"Mum? Are you here, Mum?" Aimee called as she walked from room to room. "Mum? Where are you?"

She headed for her mother's bedroom thinking she'd maybe fallen asleep, like she usually did when she'd had too much to drink. Maybe she was out cold.

"Mum, where are you?"

She entered her mother's bedroom, and her mouth dropped open.

Her mother was on the floor, lying in a pool of blood. It looked like she'd hit her head on the corner of the camphor box at the end of her bed. Aimee rushed to her mother's side and placed her fingers on the pulse in her mother's neck, checking to see if she was still alive. She'd seen it done in the movies, but it wasn't as easy to find in real life. Panicking, Aimee grabbed her mother's shoulders and shook her hard, trying to wake her up, hoping dearly everything would be okay. But her mother remained cold and still, rag doll-like.

Aimee grabbed the phone from the bedside table and dialled 000.

"I need an ambulance!" she almost shrieked down the phone, then she realised she was crying, tears trailing down her cheeks. "Mum! Mum!! Don't leave me alone! Don't you *dare* leave me alone!"

"What's your address?" the operator requested.

"Um … 284 Singleton Road, Glenglose," Aimee replied, trembling.

"We're sending an ambulance to you. It should be there in about ten minutes. Do you have anyone in the house with you?"

"No … it's just me. I think she's dead. She's very cold and not moving …"

"It's okay. Do you have a blanket you can put over her?" The operator's reassuring voice calmed Aimee.

"Yes. Yes, there's one here on the bed." Aimee pulled it down, draped it over her mother and quickly returned the phone to her ear. "What next?"

"Aimee, put your head on your mother's chest and see if you see or feel her breathing."

Aimee dropped the phone again and placed her head on her mother's chest; listened carefully for the vital signs of life. "Yes, she's breathing!" She also felt a shallow breath coming from her mother's mouth. "That means she's still alive … doesn't it?" Aimee murmured hopefully.

Then she heard the distant sound of a siren fast approaching and knew she was no longer alone. Things were going to be okay.

Racing out the front door, she waved her hands frantically at the approaching ambulance, then raced back into the house, realising she'd left the operator dangling on the other end of the phone. The ambulance drew to a halt in the driveway.

"She's in here," Aimee yelled, dragging one paramedic into the room by his shirt sleeve. Tears rolled down her cheeks. "I just found her like this when I got home … Is she going to be okay?"

"How long have you been home?" the paramedic asked

"About ten minutes," Aimee replied.

Then the paramedics took control, checking vital signs, then injecting something into Aimee's mother's arm. "This is just to keep her calm and stabilise her for the trip to the hospital." Then they lifted her mother onto a gurney and loaded it into the ambulance.

"We're going to St Valentines Memorial Hospital. Is there anybody else here with you?" the paramedic asked.

"No," Aimee replied softly. "It's just Mum and me."

"No Dad, or brothers or sisters?"

"No."

"Well, you'd better grab a change of clothes and come with us. We will try and find some accommodation for you."

Aimee hurried to her room and stuffed some clothes in a bag, then ran for the ambulance, slamming the front door shut behind her. The paramedics closed the van doors behind her as she settled onto a seat and sat staring at her mother. There were so many questions she wanted to ask but was too afraid of the answers she might get.

With sirens blaring and lights flashing, they raced towards St Valentines Hospital, which Aimee thought ironic given that her mother had never really been in love – she'd told her that one night in a morbid, drunken depression.

A short time later, the back doors were yanked open and the gurney pulled out and wheeled into the hospital. Aimee followed in silence, watching the people gathering at her mother's side, watching a large number of doctors and nurses, all clambering around to attend to her mother. They spoke a foreign language, medical terms and instructions were bandied about. In all the commotion, Aimee hovered, unsure of her role in the drama, unsure of what she should or shouldn't do next. She looked around. What was going to happen to her in all of this? What was going to happen to her mother?

"Are you Aimee Gardiner?" The voice came from behind her, and Aimee turned her head.

"Yes. Yes, I am."

"Hi. My name is Theresa Ward. I'm the hospital social worker," the lady said as she came to stand beside her. "Your mum is going to be okay. It appears she hit her head and is possibly suffering a concussion, and she'll need some staples to close the cut on her head. The doctors also want to run some tests, just to make sure everything else is okay.

"Are you hungry? Do you need a drink?" the social worker asked.

"I don't have any money," Aimee said, shaking her head. Yet she hadn't had anything since lunch and suddenly did feel hungry.

"That's okay. We can take care of it. I'll go and get us some sandwiches and some Milo. Do you like Milo?" she asked.

"It's my favourite."

"Just sit over there. I'll be back in a minute."

Theresa promptly disappeared through the glass doors at the end of the corridor, leaving Aimee to watch the hospital staff buzzing between the rooms of the hospital in organised chaos. She moved across to the designated chair and sat, still bewildered by the environment and feeling very alone.

Theresa soon returned with a tray of sandwiches and Milo, which Aimee ate slowly, still saddened and worried by her mother's ordeal. Theresa sat beside her, also watching the bustle of activity.

"I understand there's just you and your mum, and that you don't have any other relatives close by."

Aimee nodded. "Mum came up from Sydney ten years ago to get away from my dad and move into Nanna's house. But Nanna died not long after we arrived and we've been there ever since, just us."

"Do you have any friends from school you can stay with, because your mother will probably need to stay here for a few days."

Aimee shook her head. "It's okay. I can look after myself. Mum says I'm very capable. I know how to cook and clean. I'll be okay." She shrugged, not really liking the thought of being in the house on her own. "I just need to get a lift home." She looked up at Theresa proudly, to show that she was indeed capable. Her mum liked her being 'capable'.

"We have it on record that your mother has a drinking problem and that you have been left to look after yourself for a long time now. Is this true, Aimee?"

Aimee didn't like what was coming next. "I'm okay. I just need a lift …"

"It's not that simple, Aimee," Theresa said firmly. "I do understand that you wish to be independent, but legally you are not old enough to be left on your own."

Aimee shook her head. Although she cared for her mother deeply, she knew there was nothing she could do for her at the hospital.

"Aimee, unless you can give us the name of someone who can look after you for a few days, we will have to put you into foster care, and that would be with someone you do not know."

"No, not that." Aimee quickly began to think. Who could she ask? Who could possibly get her out of this mess? The only person she could think of was Sarah Brown from the riding school. But if they asked Sarah to take her, that responsibility might damage their friendship. And she didn't want that, not when she had so much going for her there. She hesitated, seeing her escape world slowly crumbling.

"Aimee, is there anybody at all?"

"Um …"

Theresa looked at her, waiting.

"Can't I just sleep here?"

"No."

And she saw her world crumbling faster. "There is a lady who might take me. Her name is Sarah Brown. She owns Trailblazers Riding School in Glenglose. I help her out on weekends, but I don't know her number."

"That's fine. I'll go and ring Sarah and explain the situation. I'll be back in a minute."

Theresa promptly disappeared through the two glass doors again, leaving Aimee feeling guilty, wondering if she had done the right thing.

By now, Aimee had grown used to strangers in white coats asking her questions about her mother's drinking problem, which, having grown up with it, didn't really see it as a problem. It was just a way of life.

Fifteen minutes passed and Theresa hurried through the two glass doors again, her smile beaming. "I've been in touch with Sarah and she's coming to get you."

With that news, Aimee felt relieved, but also scared. She had never revealed her home life to anybody, not even her school friends.

"Aimee, who has been looking after you when your mother has been ill," Theresa broke into her thoughts.

"Me. I told you, I know how to cook and clean, so it's not a problem," she said.

"Aimee, we may have to send your mother away for a few months to help her get back on the right track. If we don't help her solve her problem, she will not survive much longer. Would you like me to ask Sarah if she can care for you if that happens?"

Aimee shook her head. "Mum has always been like this. What's so different now?" Aimee asked, seeing the longer term completely destroying her friendship with Sarah. A short time might be all right, but a long time could make Sarah not want her at the stables any more.

"It is not healthy for her to drink that much alcohol, and it is not healthy for you to have that amount of responsibility."

Aimee wondered if her mother went away for help, what she would be like when she returned. Maybe things would be different.

"Aimee, hopefully, your mother will come back not relying on you so much for support, and certainly not relying on the alcohol for comfort. Hopefully, she will be capable of looking after you properly this time. It will be okay, I promise." Theresa put her arms around Aimee, the hug intended to reassure her. "Good things will come of this, you'll see."

If only, Aimee thought, feeling selfish as the image of her living with Sarah and the horses just beyond the garden slowly filtered to her mind. *Could this be the start of my dreams coming true? … even if only for a few days or weeks?*

She certainly had not imagined it happening like this. She also hoped this would be the turning point, that one day her mother would be there to share her dreams of winning. For now though, she just hoped her mother would get better and that things would soon change for the better.

Through the misty glaze of her tears, she saw a familiar face walking down the corridor towards her, the woman smiling brightly.

"Hello, Aimee," Sarah said. "How are you holding up? How is your mum?"

"Sarah Brown? Hi, I'm Theresa Ward, the hospital social

worker," Theresa interrupted. "Thank you so much for coming. May I talk to you both in my office for a moment?"

"Sure," Sarah replied, looking down at Aimee and shrugging slightly.

Once inside, Theresa shut the door behind them and began. "It is so good of you to come to Aimee's aid. Now I don't know how much you know about the family, but Aimee's mum has a serious head injury and will need to be in the hospital for a few days. We are so glad that you have offered to take Aimee into your care for that time. On top of that, however, her mother has an addiction that created this injury, and we are going to try and get her some long-term help."

Sarah sat shaking her head. "I had no idea," Sarah said, glancing at Aimee. "Aimee has never said anything about it. I can't even imagine what she's been going through."

As Aimee bowed her head with embarrassment, Sarah reached out, clasped her hand and held it tight. Then she said to Aimee softly, "We will get through this together."

"This addiction will eventually kill her if we don't intervene," Theresa went on, "so we are going to try and get her into Rehabilitation. If she will go, she will be there for at least three months."

Sarah continued to shake her head, still trying to imagine what Aimee's life had been like. "I had no idea," she finally said again. "Aimee helps me out at my riding school. I've known her for a couple of years, but rarely ever seen her mother. And Aimee has never spoken of her home life."

A slight smiled touched Theresa's lips and an eyebrow rose slightly. "I know you've agreed to take Aimee for a few days, but would you consider caring for Aimee while her mother is in rehab? There would, of course, be background checks we have to do, but if all is fine there, I would be able to arrange for financial assistance and organise the paperwork and so forth. I am really sorry to put this on you at such short notice, but we were not fully aware of Aimee's situation and its risks until tonight. Aimee doesn't have any relatives here, and it would be best if she stays close so she can still attend school and visit her mother. According to Aimee, you are the closest friend she has."

Sarah smiled widely and nodded. "Of course. I'll be Aimee's foster mum for as long as she needs me. She's a great kid."

Theresa let out a deep sigh. "That's wonderful. It really screws kids up when we have to place them where they don't know the people they will be staying with and their routine is thrown out of whack. It's a very frightening time for them." She turned towards the door. "Let's go and tell your mum the good news. I'll arrange a time to come out to you tomorrow, Sarah, and finalise the paperwork."

With the time arranged for Theresa's visit the next day, Aimee and Sarah said goodnight and headed for Aimee's house, where she collected clothes, toiletries and kissed her wall buddies goodbye for a while.

Silence reigned for a long while on the drive to Aimee's house, and Aimee could feel the wariness building between them. Sooner or later, Sarah was going to ask her about her mother. How much would she share about her mother and how much did she really have to tell? These questions fell heavy on her mind and she didn't want to answer any of them – yet.

As they reached the outskirts of the city and a billboard with a horse and rider advertising perfume whizzed by, Aimee said suddenly, "Did you hear Sally-Lee Kramer qualified for the Olympic dressage team at the last event?" She heard Sarah's loud exhale. *Was that relief?*

"No, I didn't. Who was she riding?"

And the conversation continued around the Olympic squad and the likelihood of each rider making the final selection until they turned into Aimee's street.

"Fourth house on the right," Aimee said, and, as soon as Sarah drew to a halt in the driveway, she leapt from the car. "I won't be long," she said, shutting the door and praying Sarah didn't follow her. She'd just die if Sarah saw the state of her house which she hadn't had time to clean when she'd arrived home from the stables.

Rushing inside, she gathered a few rubbish bags and stuffed her clothing into them. She placed mainly riding gear as she hoped she'd be able to ride more often while staying at Sarah's. She then realised, as an afterthought, her school uniform, shoes, backpack and homework. She stood for a moment gazing around her room – she wouldn't be waking tomorrow to her heroes on the wall but instead would be waking at Sarah's … *with my heroes outside in the paddocks.* The thought jabbed her to hurry before Sarah came looking for her.

Heading for the front door, turning out lights as she went, she snatched up a photo of her and her mum off the bench near the door and the spare set of house keys from the drawer. She understood she would have to return at some time to check the mail and clean up the mess in case anyone came to check on her. Outside on the path, she turned back to the now dark house, the fear of what was to become of her in the long-term creeping in: what if her mother didn't get well? Then she turned to the car, where Sarah sat waiting, peering through the windscreen at her. She looked worried.

"Aimee. It has just occurred to me. How well do you know your neighbours?" Sarah gingerly asked.

"Mr and Mrs Carter? They are the most wonderful people, and they are very caring. Why do you ask?" Aimee responded.

"We need to have a chat with them and explain the situation. Let's ask them if they wouldn't mind collecting the mail and looking after the house for us so that your place doesn't look deserted. It is too late to do it now. We shall pop back in the morning and meet with them. Are you okay with that? We'll also collect the mail from them occasionally so that your bills can be paid. I'll talk to Theresa about that problem. We can work this out together," Sarah explained.

Aimee nodded. With a glazed stare, she looked straight at Sarah.

"Are you okay?" Sarah asked as Aimee settled in for the journey back to the riding school.

Aimee again nodded. "Yeah," she sighed.

For the moment, she was fine. She'd be staying at Sarah's with her beloved horses right outside the door, and Sarah was dealing with any pending problems the vacant house might pose.

Chapter 3

The New Life

On arriving back at Trailblazers, Sarah ushered Aimee to the bedroom she would use during her stay, a room decorated exactly as Aimee would have liked her own room to be – a frilly white bedspread on the single bed, a white desk and chair, and a pine bookcase against one wall with an assortment of horse books decorating the shelves. On the walls were photos of Sarah, displaying her numerous wins in her younger years, which Aimee wished were photos of herself in the same situation. She sighed deeply as she turned, taking in every aspect of her new private space, a slight thought niggling as to why Sarah had such an elaborately decorated room when she didn't have a daughter of her own. Her head tilted slightly as she turned back to Sarah and frowed. "Do you have a daughter?"

Sarah shrugged and smiled tightly. "No." An awkward silence passed between them as Aimee fully appreciated the pristine room and its welcoming warmth. How she could get used to this!

"Well, put your stuff away in the drawers and cupboard, and I'll fix you something to eat. Are you hungry?"

"Starving," Aimee grinned, "… as long as it's not inconvenient."

"It's not. Pastie slice and chips coming up," Sarah said.

"What?" Aimee asked, frowning again.

"Pasties. You know, meat and vegetable wrapped in pastry.

Have you never had one before?" Sarah asked as she headed to the door.

'No, I don't think so … but I'm game enough to try anything."

"Okay, it won't be long. Help yourself to a drink or the television, and I'll get dinner started."

The meal was soon ready, and Aimee sat opposite Sarah enjoying a nutritious home-cooked meal, something she'd not had for a very long time. When she'd finished eating, out of habit Aimee immediately rose, took her plate to the sink and started to fill the sink to do the dishes.

"Leave those, sweetie. You must be very tired. Why don't you go off and have a shower and get ready for bed. We really need to sit down and have a chat about things, but right now I think you need a good night's sleep."

Aimee's back tightened as she stood at the sink. As much as Sarah was helping her, she really didn't want her to know about her life outside of Trailblazers; she didn't want to feel embarrassed or have to explain what her life had been like. A shower and bed sounded like a good idea to avoid that conversation so she nodded.

"The bathroom is the third door on the left. Towels are in the cupboard."

"Thank you. And thank you for doing this for me," Aimee said as she turned to head for the bathroom. Silently, she said, *thank you for not asking me questions tonight. I really don't want to remember it.*

Aimee enjoyed her shower, dressed in a long, loose, horse-motif t-shirt that was her pyjamas and went out to say goodnight to Sarah. "What time do you get up in the morning … I would like to help feed the horses?"

"You can have a sleep in," Sarah smiled. "You will need all your energy tomorrow. Goodnight, sweetie."

With that, Aimee climbed into bed, curled up to her soft sweet-smelling pillow and dreamed of the adventures that lay ahead of her at Trailblazers.

Chapter 4

The New Adventure

Aimee woke after a deep, pleasant night's sleep, and immediately became disorientated in her new surroundings. But soon, the lovely scene around her brought back the events of the previous night and she realised where she was. Instantly, she swung out of bed, rummaged through her drawers to find her best riding clothes, trying to remember which drawer she'd put everything in. Satisfied with the selection, she dressed and hurried from the room to help Sarah feed up. But Sarah was sitting at the dining table enjoying her morning cup of coffee and a piece of toast.

"Good morning. Did you sleep well?" she asked.

"I did, but I should go and feed the horses," Aimee said.

"Relax. I've already done them. You can give me a hand in getting them ready for the busy day ahead," she smiled. "What would you like for breakfast?"

Aimee sat down to a large bowl of cereal and two pieces of toast and vegemite. For the first time she could ever remember, someone was looking after her, and she enjoyed the change. Yet she felt somewhat guilty at not being independent. Then the thought crossed her mind: had she been at home yesterday instead of enjoying herself at the stables, would her mother have been injured? Guilt suddenly washed over her, but she quickly broke that thought by thinking about all of the jobs that had to be done before the first lesson – it was something she had taught herself to do: focus on something else to stay positive; it was the only way she had been able to cope.

After breakfast, Aimee and Sarah wandered down to the stables and began the morning ritual of preparing the horses for the nine o'clock lessons.

"Aimee, I need Rinso, Barney, Bubbles and Tonka for the first lesson. Could you get them ready please?"

Aimee quickly headed off to the tack room, where she lifted down each pony's gear and placed it out ready for the riders to saddle up when they arrived. Ensuring the stirrups were properly run up and bridle reins folded to avoid trip hazards, she tied each pony in its appropriate place and placed the sturdy boxes nearby should some children not be tall enough to lift the saddle onto their mount's back. Then she grabbed the bucket and wheelbarrow and started cleaning the stalls. This was one of those unpleasant jobs she knew had to be done, and Sarah had taught her much could be learnt about the horse's health during the cleaning process, so she stayed vigilant.

The ten stalls took her about an hour to finish – just in time to watch the eleven o'clock lesson. This lesson was special because they were all practising for the district dressage championships being held at the local Pony club grounds the following Sunday. Aimee hoped she could go with Sarah to watch them and that way learn the formalities of riding a dressage competition. Sarah would certainly need a hand to load up the horses and ponies and off-load them at the pony club grounds for the riders who borrowed mounts from Trailblazers. That meant Sarah would also need help in saddling up. *Oh I do hope she asks me to go? And I do hope she doesn't ask Mum to give permission.*

Eleven o'clock came around a lot sooner than she expected, and she quickly stowed the tools away and hurried to the arena to watch the girls, all about her age, embark on their dreams.

Aimee had studied the Preliminary and Novice dressage tests

numerous times, especially during her maths lessons at school, and she knew every movement of each test off by heart. This made following the girl's tests easier, especially when they made a mistake and went the wrong way. Although Aimee was not actually riding the test, being on the sidelines, she still felt the growing excitement.

The lesson finished quickly, and Aimee returned to the stables to help with the lunchtime chores of wiping down the tack, airing the saddle blankets and feeding the horses. Then Sarah clamped a grip on Aimee's shoulder and turned her towards the house.

"It's our lunchtime," she announced, and she, Karen and Aimee headed to the kitchen. Aimee pulled various sandwich fillings out of the fridge; Sarah raided the drink fridge for cold cans of soda, and Karen fetched the plates, bread and butter. All three concocted sandwiches to their liking as Sarah explained to Karen a little of the events of the previous night, and that Aimee was, for now, a permanent part of the team. Karen rose and hugged Aimee consolingly, making Aimee blush with embarrasment – for the first time in her life she actually felt wanted, not just needed.

"Aimee, would you like to ride Monnie in the two o'clock lesson today?" Sarah asked, one fine eyebrow rrising in expectation.

"Oh yes, please," Aimee replied, a grin widely spreading.

At that prospect, Aimee devoured her lunch so she could go and prepare her champion horse for another lesson, Sarah and Karen following her more leisurely back to the stables.

Aimee's lesson went exceptionally well, with Monnie accomplishing the most precise simple changes in two trot strides in response to Aimee's aids and Aimee patted her profusely. Monnie had been bred to be Sarah's next champion dressage horse and was rising through the levels when Sarah had an accident that had limited her ability to ride. She had, however, told Aimee after that first ride a year ago, she had educated Monnie enough to give Aimee the flying start she needed to succeed, and Aimee and Monnie had just clicked. Both Sarah and Aimee were delighted with their progress, Sarah stating during one weekend lesson that, if Aimee intended to compete, Monnie was the one she should ride.

The final pupil left at 6.00 pm and Rinso, the last horse working, was put to bed for a well-earned rest. When all the horses looked contented munching their night feed, they returned to the house for a much-needed shower and meal.

Sadly, Aimee realised the weekend was over. She had school the next day, and wondered if even school would appear better now with the change of environment.

Monday morning Aimee rose extra early so she could help with the chores before school.

"Good morning, Sarah," she greeted cheerfully as she caught up to Sarah at the stables. "I'll make up the feeds if you like and start putting them in."

Sarah looked up from placing buckets down and smiled. "You sure can, hon. Then you'd better hightail it back to the house and get ready for school."

"Okay," Aimee replied and started doling out feed into the appropriate buckets.

Breakfast came and went, and Aimee and Sarah slid into the car and drove to the high school to inform the principal of the new situation. Although Aimee felt comfortable with Sarah, she was unsure how the school would accept the dramatic change — they had never been made aware of the situation at home. Being self-sufficient, she had hid the situation well.

Sarah approached the front reception and asked to speak with the principal, Mrs Simpson, a tall, elegant lady with soft brown eyes.

"Good morning, Aimee. How are you today?" she asked. "Mrs Gardiner, I presume," she added, turning to Sarah.

"Ah, no. I am Sarah Brown … I was wondering if I may have a word with you."

Mrs Simpson ushered them into her office, where Sarah explained that Aimee's mother had suffered a nasty head injury and that Aimee would be staying with her for the time being.

"Oh, Aimee, I am so sorry," Mrs Simpson exclaimed. "How hard that would have been to deal with. You are a very brave girl."

Unwilling to divulge anything further, Sarah advised that the school would soon receive notification from Child Services confirming this in writing.

"That is fine. Thank you for telling us. Aimee, if there is anything we can do for you, please don't hesitate to ask. Even if you just need someone to talk to, we will always be available for you."

With that, Sarah left her details with the school administrator at the front counter, and Aimee said goodbye to Sarah and Mrs Simpson and headed for class as the first siren had sounded. She felt immensely grateful that Sarah had not blurted out the whole story, therefore keeping her pride intact. She would hate anyone to know how she lived.

Her fifteenth birthday was in a few days, and Aimee now realised that, with her mother in the hospital, any hope of her hinting for items she would need to fulfil her dream of competing was now dead. The thought hit home bitterly, but she swallowed her disappointment: it would not be the first time she'd had her hopes dashed. Sometimes her mother didn't remember her birthday at all until months later. Regardless of how it hurt though, she didn't want Sarah to know how she felt:

she was already an imposition. So, she held her heartache close and tried not to let her emotions falter when Sarah was around.

"What is the matter, Aimee?" Sarah asked as they fed the horses in the evening. "What's bothering you?"

"Nothing," Aimee muttered. "I'm fine."

"Sure, sure," Sarah replied, standing up from her task and watching Aimee closely. "Anything happen at school today?"

Aimee thought quickly. "I only got a B in English and not an A." It wasn't a lie.

"But that's fantastic," Sarah replied. "I am very proud of you for getting a B. Don't be too hard on yourself."

If only she knew the truth, Aimee thought, her lips pursing tightly at the bitter taste the lie left in her mouth.

"And a B is not going to change the beautiful person you are," Sarah added. "You have to realise you've had a lot on your mind lately and I know you are concerned about your mother. Would you like to go and visit her tomorrow?"

"Oh yes please! I do hope she's okay."

"I am sure she will be. She's getting the best of care where she is."

They continued with their tasks, Aimee thoroughly enjoying the routine of the life she was settling into.

Chapter 5

An Unhappy Feeling

Visiting the hospital was not a pleasant experience for Aimee – so many sick people in the same place bothered her, even though she knew they were there to be made well again.

She and Sarah eventually found Room 202 at the end of the long corridor and wandered quietly along to Bed C where Aimee's mother lay. Her mother's head was wrapped in bandages and tubes were attached to her arm. Aimee almost gasped but contained it; instead, she gave her mother a kiss and a hug. "Hello, Mum. This is Sarah who is looking after me while you are in here. Sarah owns the riding school. We are having so much fun. Are you getting better?"

Her mother looked tired, her eyes bloodshot. "Thank you very much for looking after Aimee for me," she said weakly. "I really appreciate how happy you have made her." Then she looked at Aimee. "I'm so sorry, Aimee. I hope you will forgive me," she exclaimed.

"Yes, of course, I will. You're alive … that's the main thing."

Aimee had heard this speech many times and locked this latest one into her memory bank. She sat hoping her mother would mention her birthday so maybe Sarah would make a cake without her saying anything. But sadly, this didn't happen and, after thirty minutes of extracted conversation, Aimee and Sarah left her mother to rest.

"Goodbye, Mum. I'll pop in and see you soon. You hurry up

and get well. Love you heaps," she said as she moved towards the door.

With that sad departure, Aimee and Sarah headed for the car, feeling relieved to be on their way home.

"How about take-away?" Sarah asked. "Your pick."

"You mean like hamburgers and chips?" Aimee asked, grinning.

"You have not had many take-aways, have you, Aimee?"

"No," Aimee replied, feeling like she should have.

Still disappointed at the prospect of a dull birthday, she ate her chicken without much enthusiasm yet quietly enjoyed the newfound crispy taste.

"How long has your Mum had that condition?" Sarah suddenly asked as they sat in the car in the car park.

Aimee swallowed her last chip. "About ten years … just after my mum left dad." She shrugged. "I've learnt to live without him as I never really got to know him, but Mum was another issue. She never seemed to get over him."

"Oh … so you've survived on your own for all this time?" Sarah asked cautiously.

"Not always. Mum would come good occasionally, for about three weeks or so, then she'd be back at it again. She would always have money in her purse, so I would pinch it and go and buy some food and pay what bills I could pay at the Post Office. It's amazing what you learn when you have to."

"How come the school never found out?"

Aimee smiled to herself. "I always made my lunch and washed my clothes. A couple of years ago, I learnt how to iron them, but by that stage, everybody had assumed I was a scruffy kid, so they just accepted it. I never had a friend over, so no one ever knew."

"You are absolutely amazing, Aimee." Sarah shook her head. "How are you coping with the change?" she then asked.

"I feel like a kid again," Aimee admitted, smiling down at her chicken. "It's so nice having someone take care of me – even if I don't feel I need it. But thank you for doing this for me, Sarah. I really do appreciate it."

"You're welcome." Sarah smiled, and gave Aimee's shoulder a gentle shove.

They soon returned home and finished the night with a warm cup of Milo and a mutually appreciated hug.

Though still disheartened at missing another birthday, Aimee now felt very much loved, which made up for everything.

Chapter 6

Tears of Joy

Two days later, Aimee turned over and opened her eyes, her smile slowly spreading as she scanned the room. She had not slept well, her first thoughts dallying through the night that she would wake another year older; she was now fifteen and living in the ideal situation, and wishing that her mum could be just like Sarah.

Realising that she'd overslept, she rose and ambled to the kitchen, annoyed that Sarah would have finished the horses by now.

"Good morning, birthday girl!" Sarah greeted her, her smile beaming. "Would you like to open your presents now or when you get home from school?"

Aimee's jaw dropped open, and her eyes widened. Her heart started doing little flips. "What? Oh … oh yes. Yes, please. Now? Now! Oh thank you, Sarah … thank you so much. I didn't think you knew."

"I made a point of finding out," Sarah said, grinning and tapping a finger on her temple. She turned and gathered up an armful of presents from the sideboard and placed them on the table.

One by one, Aimee opened each present, a lump forming in her throat that there were so many. Her eyes moistened further as she peeled the paper away from each item. First, she unwrapped a pair of cream jodhpurs, then a smaller parcel, a black button-up vest. From the next she withdrew a crisp white shirt and black tie. A medium-sized square box held a helmet, already fitted with a black slip over cover like the dressage competitors wore. She turned to the two large boxes, her hands starting to shake as each gift out-did the previous one, each present beginning to form the overall picture Sarah had devised. She could barely stop her hands trembling as she peeled back the paper of the first long box, the outline of long black leather boots pasted on the side causing tears to roll down her cheek. Her eyes blurred so she could barely see and her nose began to run. Sarah handed her the tissue box, smiling widely.

"Come on, open the last one," she urged.

Her eyes brimming with moisture, making Sarah a blur in her vision, Aimee reached for the last box. "Oh, Sarah, you didn't have to … this is too …"

"Come on, open the box," Sarah insisted excitedly.

Aimee's fingers peeled away the sticky tape, pulled back the layer of bright green paper. It was a plain white box. Sarah helped pull the paper out of the way as Aimee lifted the corner of the lid and peered into its darkened space. Her face felt wet as tears streamed down both cheeks, and her hand covered her mouth to stop her sobs escaping.

Easing the lid aside, she reached in and lifted out the tailored black jacket, her words of gratitude locking in her throat, almost choking her. She had every piece of riding attire required to compete with the other girls. This was the best birthday ever!!

She looked at Sarah as she wiped away the tears and reached for the tissues, a deep inhale unlocking her words. "Sarah, these are so beautiful. I am so … so …"

Sarah moved forward and hugged her. "I know," she said softly. "Oh, but there's more …" She pulled an envelope from the sideboard and handed it to her.

Not the usual shape for a birthday card, Aimee thought as

she opened the envelope. And she was right. It wasn't a card. It was a letter, personally addressed to Miss Aimee Gardiner.

Dear Miss Gardiner,

This letter confirms your entry in the Preliminary 1C and the Novice 2B on Sunday, the 10th of March 2013, riding Monique.

Your times are as follows:
- Preliminary 1C 10.30 am
- Novice 2B 11.20 am

We wish you all the best and hope you have a great day.

Yours truly

D. Kinnon

Debbie Kinnon
Secretary

Tears streamed down Aimee's face again, and she wrapped her arms around Sarah's neck and held on tight. Her every dream had come true this very morning and she was the luckiest teenager in the world.

For three weeks, Aimee practised and practised under Sarah's watchful eye, her mentor making sure she was thoroughly prepared. The day before the event, Aimee spent washing Monnie and trimming her tail, feathers and coronet band. She cleaned all her gear, checked all the stitching to ensure it was in good order and would pass the gear check, checked it again. Then she packed the car and the horse float and made sure Monnie had enough feed to last her the whole day. She was ready for her big day of competion.

Laying in bed that night, Aimee continually went through the test in her head. *Visualise it, see yourself riding every movement, confidently and precisely.* She'd not been allowed to ride it over and over in case Monnie became bored, so they had ridden the movements, and practiced the whole test only three times over a number of days. And now she lay picturing herself as a top dressage rider, flowing through the whole test with grace and precision. She spent an hour doing the Preliminary test, then did the same with the Novice till she felt comfortable – then she realised she couldn't remember the first test. And tossed and turned, her stomach churning.

What if I forget the test? Sarah will be so disappointed in me, and I will let Monnie down. Eventually, she slept uneasily and on waking visualised the Preliminary test again. She did remember it! Smiling, she swung out of bed, even though the sun hadn't yet come up. Sunday had finally arrived.

Breakfast was a rushed affair as she and Sarah still had horses to feed and let out before they left for the show. Aimee gulped down the last of her Milo, pulled on her boots and hurried down to Monnie's stall to make sure she was okay and still clean. The mare, snugly wrapped in warm stable rugs, nickered as she arrived. Aimee breathed with relief: she'd had an awful feeling something might have happened during the night to prevent her riding in her first competition.

"We'll put them all out and feed them in the paddocks," Sarah said as she mixed the feeds in the shed. "Feeds in first, then we'll lead them down."

Sarah said as she shut the last gate, "Okay, Miss, up to the house and put on your riding clothes, put a tracksuit on over the top and put your jacket in the car. Then I'll braid your hair."

On the drive to the showgrounds, Sarah looked across at Aimee and smiled. "You look wonderful," she said, "and you've got Monnie gleaming. Do you remember your test?"

"I'm so nervous. I can remember the Prelim, but now I've forgotten the Novice," Aimee wailed. "I do hope I don't muck it up."

"You only have to remember the Preliminary for now. Focus on that. There is a break between the two tests, so you have time to focus on the Novice then. You'll be fine. What you are feeling is normal for a first competition, and a second and third and fourth … and …"

They both glanced at each other and grinned, and Aimee relaxed. By the time they arrived at the competition, she felt rather composed, her nerves diminishing as she got down to business. She needed to warm Monnie up for at least fifteen minutes before riding the actual test, so she had to be mounted in about half an hour. In that time, she had stripped Monnie's rugs and brushed her till she glistened. Sarah had plaited Monnie's mane and tail earlier so all Aimee had to do was saddle her up and don her helmet and jacket. She felt so professional as she stood checking her reflection in the car window.

"Monnie and Aimee, you both look a million dollars," Sarah gushed as she came around from behind the float.

"I just hope I do well," Aimee replied, dearly hoping she would make Sarah proud and do Monnie justice.

"You just go out there and have fun," Sarah insisted, her hand on Aimee's helmet giving Aimee's whole body a shake. It was just what Aimee had needed.

Sarah pulled the stirrup irons down the leathers and snapped them twice to ensure they were well connected to the saddle, then she slid Monnie's reins over her head and pushed Aimee into position. Then she legged her up into the saddle. Pulling a rag from her back pocket, she wiped the dust off Aimee's boots and stood back to examine the pair standing in front of her. "You look two million dollars. Now go out there and do your thing, just as I have shown you." She gave Aimee a double thumbs up then stepped out of the way. "This is so exciting!"

It was all up to Aimee now.

As there was no numbering system, Aimee headed down the warm up area and kept listening for her name as she put Monnie through suppling exercises at walk, trot and canter. She would have to present herself to the steward as soon as her name was called to avoid being disqualified.

Finally, her moment arrived, and she almost froze as she heard her name bellowed out by the gear checker. Taking three deep breaths, she turned Monnie and walked briskly to the official to have her gear inspected. This she knew would be no problem as she had checked the gear three times already, and Sarah had checked it again once she had mounted. She felt immaculate in the new riding outfit Sarah had bought her. It must have cost her a fortune and she therefore had to do extremely well to show Sarah it had been worth it.

Her gear check completed, the lady commenting to Aimee that she and Monnie 'looked lovely', Aimee watched the rider ahead of her riding the test to again visualise where to go and at what pace. Then it was her moment of glory. Her stomach starting to feel strangely unsettled, Aimee gathered Monnie up beneath her and nudged her down to the judge's car at the C end of the arena. She waited, her nerves starting to wriggle inside her. The judge who was sitting scoring up the previous test looked like a kind lady, and who, when she wound down her window, seemed to sense this was Aimee's first time.

"Aimee Gardiner?" she asked, sizing up the young girl on the huge black horse. Aimee nodded meekly. "I will toot my horn when you get to the other end, and you will have sixty seconds to start your test. Are you ready?"

"Yes … I think so," Aimee said quietly, right at that moment not feeling as if she really was. *But really all you have to do is remember the test,* she reminded herself. *And ride like Sarah. Ride like a champion.*

"Good luck," the judge replied.

Aimee turned Monnie and trotted back to the A end of the arena, images of the test running through her mind. She was thankful Monnie had competed many times before and was pleased how smooth she felt beneath her. She commenced circling to one side of the arena, like Sarah had taught her, made sure she was on the correct rein to make a straight line down the centre line; she concentrated on Monnie's rhythm, on the roundness of her circle, on her own position. Then, like a sudden jolt of lightning, the car horn barped. Aimee shuddered, then lifted her chin, eased in a deep breath and lined up with the centre line as she completed her circle, and began the fulfilment of her dream.

All the words Sarah had spoken came back to her now as Monnie trotted rhythmically down the centre line to X. *Sit tall; stretch down into halt, and breathe. And visualise – you are a champion. You are a champion.* The butterflies settled in her stomach and she nudged Monnie gently to move on, making every movement supple, every aid precise. *Look up and look where you are going* – and when she did, Monnie followed her line. It was like riding by mental telepathy. Sarah had said it would be like that when everything fell into place. Think it and it will happen. Finally, she was turning down centre line and heading for X again, and the final salute. It was almost over, just like that. She was astounded: the test was finished so quickly. She was at the final halt, Monnie squaring up to stand balanced on all four feet. Bowing her head and lowering her hand, Aimee saluted the judge. She had done it! Her smile spread wide. Then she remembered to breathe again, and to stay calm so Monnie maintained a steady loose rein walk out of the arena.

Then she was out through A.

Sarah's face beamed as Aimee rode towards her. "I did it,

Sarah. I did it!"

"You did it beautifully, sweetie. You looked so elegant out there."

"Really?"

"Really! You should score pretty high. Now come on, back to the car. You need to focus on the Novice test now," and she fell into step beside Monnie.

"How long have I got?"

"About half an hour. Step down and have a drink, run through the test in your mind. I'll water Monnie," and she led the black mare away to the back of the float

Aimee sat on the float's wheel arch and tried to settle her nerves, which had suddenly resurfaced. This next test was harder than the last one, and she would have to ride Monnie stronger and more accurately than before. She was doing her deep breathing exercises when Sarah returned with Monnie.

"Okay, it's time. Good luck again," Sarah said as she legged Aimee up onto the saddle.

"Thanks, Sarah," Aimee replied as she rode off toward the arena.

Either the half-hour was very quick, or there were a few scratchings as Aimee heard her name called sooner than expected. She felt relieved that Monnie appeared ready to work again. She reported to the gear checker, as she had done previously, and patiently waited to be signalled to go to the judge. In the spare minutes, she assessed the quality of the rider in the arena, weighing up her competition. Then just as before, another bolt of lightning, her name was called, alerting her to present herself to the judge. Although it happened so quickly, after her first test, Aimee felt confident she would ride this one well.

As the previous competitor left the arena, she rode down to the judge as before, and received the standard instruction, this time by a different judge. As Aimee commenced circling at the A end, she felt more relaxed, like she'd done this many times before. Breathing in and out, she focused on the moments ahead, visualised, and when the horn blasted the air, she rode a smooth curve, straightened Monnie up and aimed for the centre line between the A markers.

Blinking softly as she entered the arena at trot, in her mind she became Isabelle Werth, world-renowned Olympic rider. She breathed in and out, felt taller, lighter, more balanced, like she was riding the Grand Prix test in the Olympics, Monnie, her superbly experienced black mare looking dazzling as the sun gleamed off her coat.

Aimee saluted at X, and commenced her test at trot, Monnie beneath her swinging freely along. As Isabelle Werth would, she made her transitions precisely, Monnie given the aids at the exact moment to execute the changes right at the markers; she rode her corners deeper, curving Monnie around her inside leg; made her circles smoother. Monnie's canter felt like she was floating. Stretching taller and easing her inside shoulder back for the final turn down centre line, Aimee came back into herself. She was now Aimee Gardiner again, and she had just ridden her first Novice test ever, and she loved it!

Smiling widely, she breathed out softly and Monnie squared herself in the halt at G and lowered the tension in her rounded frame. With a gracious salute to the judge, Aimee eased the rein and let Monnie walk the corner, accurately as the test was not yet over, then loose rein walked her across the diagonal to A in a nice rhythmic pace.

Aimee's smile broadened, and a tear touched her eye. This had been her dream for so, so long she could not believe she was here; she could not even believe she was dressed like a champion rider. Oh how she loved Sarah and Monnie for making her dreams come true.

She patted Monnie's neck profusely as she exited the arena, and ambled back to the float, feeling very relaxed and very proud to have completed the test as she had. It had all felt so right.

With no more tests to ride that day, Aimee swung down from the saddle and focused on making Monnie more comfortable. First, she took off the bridle and saddle then tossed a light rug over her back until she could brush her down. She fetched the kit needed to undo the plaits and snipped and carefully unwound each delicate rosette along the mare's neck, combing out the curls and wetting the mane to lie flat again. Then she removed the rug and brushed the sleek coat that had sweated only slightly under the saddle. She rewarded Monnie with a bucket of water and racked up a hay net just as Sarah came back to the float.

"They have some really good riders here today," Sarah told her as she checked Monnie was tied up correctly. "But you looked really good too. It's the best I've seen you ride."

It felt the best she had ever ridden too, Aimee realised. She had been floating, Monnie pre-empting the signals before she'd applied them. It had seemed like they'd been one, and she wondered if that was what it was like to ride like a world champion.

In the midst of her dreaming, the bellowing of the loudspeaker broke through her thoughts.

"We have the results of the Preliminary 1C test."

To Aimee, this announcement seemed to take forever.

"In first place … Aimee Gardiner on Monique

In second place … Susan Player on Toontown

In third place … Justine Rogers on Trustworthy

In fourth place … Louise Hillcrest on Barney Rubble

Fifth place … Donna Smith on Respectfully Yours, and

In sixth place is Jane Turner on Bank Buster.

"Would all of those riders please come to the clubhouse to

collect your prizes and tests. Congratulations to all."

"You did it, Aimee! You did it! Well done. I am so proud of you." Sarah clutched Aimee in an enormous bear hug, tears running down her cheeks.

Aimee smiled quietly in disbelief. Quickly checking that Monnie was safe to leave, Sarah gripped Aimee's arm. "Come on, let's go get your prize. I am so excited," while Aimee, still smiling, tried to fathom if she'd heard it correctly.

Having never before been the centre of attention, Aimee felt uneasy. While she did not find it daunting, a fearful thought wondered when the bubble would burst, a bubble she wanted to enjoy for as long as she could. But it would burst, sometime.

As they reached the clubhouse, the loudspeaker bellowed once again.

"Your attention, please. We have the results of the Novice 2B test. They are as follows:

In first place … Aimee Gardiner on Monique

Second place … Louise Hillcrest on Barney Rubble

In third place … Susan Player on Toontown

In fourth place … Robert Redcliffe on Rusty

Fifth place is Mary Bottler on Just for Me, and

in sixth place … Jane Turner on Bank Buster. Congratulations to all of you."

Another round of hugs and kisses and Aimee's dream exploded into reality. Her bubble now floated up higher and higher.

Chapter 7

A Joy to Remember

Rejoicing filled the car on the trip home.

"I still can't believe it, Sarah," Aimee gushed, holding up her ribbons. "I still can't believe it." Then she paused. "It wasn't just a dream, was it?"

Sarah laughed. "No. It certainly wasn't a dream. And this calls for a celebration I think. … What's your favourite chocolate?"

"Anything, as long as there's lots of it," Aimee said with a cheeky grin and a glint in her eye.

Sarah pulled over at the nearest shop and headed for the chocolate section where she couldn't decide what flavour to buy so bought many. One block had disappeared before they pulled into the driveway.

After parking the car and off-loading Monnie, Sarah unpacked, wiped over the gear and put everything away while Aimee ensured Monnie was put comfortably to bed and given her well-deserved dinner, all the while giving her an abundance of hugs.

"Well, I don't know about you, my little champion," Sarah said as she poked her head over Monnie's stable door, checking that the mare was fully tended, "but I am ready for a warm shower, a bite to eat and a nice cozy bed – it's been a long day, and I don't think you're far behind me."

Aimee wrapped her arms once more around Monnie's neck and kissed her goodnight. "I am still on Cloud Nine," she murmured. "I think I'll float across to the house. I simply cannot remember a happier day in my life and I don't think I will sleep a wink."

They headed to the house, where Aimee hung two new decorations in her room. The blue ribbons undoubtedly took pride of place, until the next big win. Then she focussed on the next task at hand – getting ready for school the following day. For once, Aimee had some special news to tell her friends.

Although still excited about her riding achievement, Aimee wondered whether to tell her mother during their weekly visit – her mother had never shared her enthusiasm for riding, and she felt at times she resented it.

Wednesday afternoon arrived too soon and Sarah met Aimee in the school car park, ready to take her to see her mother.

Aimee's mother, now in her eighth week of rehabilitation, looked better than she had in a long time, and Aimee realised she had made some wonderful progress. She also made eye contact with her now, which Aimee noticed immediately. But clearly, there was still a long way to go.

"Mum, Sarah has been fantastic," Aimee blurted out. "She's been spoiling me rotten. I'm so lucky, aren't I."

Aimee's mother glanced over them both. "I'm so glad to see you so happy. So tell me all the things you've been up to."

Aimee flashed a quick look at Sarah for approval. "Mum, I did my first dressage day last Sunday on Sarah's best horse, Monnie. I came first in my two tests, Mum. My first tests ever and I won both. I am so happy."

Sarah sat silent. This was Aimee's story; Aimee's visit.

"That's fabulous. Well done," her mother replied drily. Then she looked over to Sarah. "Thank you for providing Aimee the opportunity to compete. I will pay you for your time when I am out of here," she added just as dully.

Sarah ignored her tone. "You're welcome, Rachael, and no payment is required. Your daughter is a very talented young lady who deserved the wins."

After an hour of idle conversation, Aimee noticed her mum looked tired and they ended the visit. "Mum, please get better soon," Aimee said. "I miss you so much."

"I will, my darling. I am trying to, for your sake."

With that, Aimee gave her mother a warm hug and kissed her goodbye, and she and Sarah left the hospital. They drove past by Aimee's house to collect the mail and checked that everything was okay. Everything appeared to be in order and Aimee felt relieved there was nothing she had to deal with – it was as it was after she and Sarah had cleaned it from top to bottom a few weeks earlier.

Having grown up in this house, Aimee felt sad returning to it, as she now often wondered where she really belonged.

They arrived home in time to quickly secure the horses in their stables and feed them, then they headed for the kitchen where they prepared a meal together and sat down to enjoy the well-deserved steak and salad dinner.

With each passing week, Aimee and Sarah grew closer, and began to comfortably reveal more about their lives to each other. Aimee began to wish that Sarah was her real mother, but guilt quickly put a stop to any further thoughts on that.

One night, Aimee asked the question that had troubled her since her arrival. "Sarah, my bedroom was all set up before I arrived. How did you know I was coming to you?"

"I didn't," Sarah replied. "I have always had that room set up. It's for my daughter who would be about your age now. Her name is Marjorie."

"You talk as if she's still around," Aimee noted, frowning.

Sarah hedged and looked uncomfortable. Then she sighed.

"Like your mother, Aimee, I had a drinking problem many, many years ago. I was totally out of control. Unfortunately, I fell pregnant and had to put my baby up for adoption as I was not capable of caring for her. I haven't seen her since she was born."

"Why the room then?" Aimee frowned deeper.

"I guess deep down I had hoped she would walk back into my life some day. But, having you in my life now has made me very happy too."

"Me too," Aimee smiled slightly, and left the conversation there – it had obviously hit a sad place for Sarah.

"Time for bed, young lady, as you have school tomorrow," Sarah said, "and you also have to work Monnie tomorrow as you have the District Dressage Day coming up in three weeks."

Aimee kissed Sarah good night and fell into bed to dream of adding another blue ribbon to her collection.

Chapter 8

A New Challenge

Months later.

Working Monnie under Sarah's expert eye was the best part of coming home from school, and Aimee spent many hours practising and refining her skills ready for the next big competition. Even with this much practice though, the quality of competitors she would be up against sent the butterflies in her stomach soaring. Their squirming kept her awake some nights until she learnt to calm them by visualising riding like a champion, like she had in her first Novice test. 'To become a champion,' Sarah had said, 'you must first see yourself as a champion.'

On Wednesday afternoon, Sarah collected Aimee from school for her weekly visit to the hospital. On the way, Aimee piped up and asked, "Do you think Mum would be able to come and watch me ride on Sunday?" She had been thinking about it all day, and how nice it would be for her mother to see her competing.

"You can only ask, Aimee. You never know ... she may be able to get a pass for the day. Would you like her to stay overnight with us so that she can come with us?" Sarah reluctantly asked.

"Um, let's just see if she can come first," Aimee replied, feeling a little uncomfortable about the concept.

"Hello, Mum. How are you today?" Aimee asked as she reached her mother's bedside.

"Hello, sweetheart. Hello, Sarah. I'm doing fine. How are you both this week?" Rachael continued, sounding more confident. She also looked better this week and appeared to have been given more independence in looking after herself.

"Mum," Aimee hesitated, "… I am riding in a dressage competition on Sunday and … we were wondering if you would be allowed out to come and watch me ride."

Aimee sat on the nearby chair, hanging on the response her mother was about to give her.

"I don't think so, darling. I don't think I'm ready for the big wide world yet. But thank you for asking. You will let me know how you go. Please … I would love to know," she continued.

"That's okay, Mum. I understand. Maybe next time."

Slightly disappointed, Aimee went on to discuss school events and spent the next half hour asking about what was happening in the hospital and about her mother's progress. She then said goodbye and kissed her mother on the cheek and confirmed her visit the following Wednesday.

Rachael said goodbye and watched them disappear down the corridor for another week, looking up and smiling as a nurse came into the room. "My daughter is riding in a dressage competition on Sunday," she said, beaming.

"Oh, that's lovely. Would you like to go and watch her?" came the reply.

Rachael shook her head. "Oh no. I don't think so."

The big day finally arrived. This time, Aimee was riding against the 'Big Guys', competitors who had already had a taste of success at this level. She hoped she didn't make a fool of herself. She had her two favourite tests to ride again. The

Preliminary 1C and the Novice 2B. Although she knew them off by heart, her performance had to be even more polished than before. She was also aware that the first two placegetters from each test would gain a position in the National team to compete in the Junior National championship the following year. Aimee wanted to make her mother so proud, even though she would not be there physically.

"Aimee, it's time to mount up. Your first test is in three-quarters of an hour and you need to warm Monnie up," Sarah reminded her. Aimee felt the butterflies in her stomach rapidly reproducing, forming their own colony.

"Okay," she said meekly as she finished pulling up Monnie's girth.

"Good luck, sweetheart," Sarah said, and she gave Aimee a final hug. "Be careful not to warm her up too much, otherwise you'll make her look dull," she continued.

"Sure," was Aimee's quick response.

Aimee entered the warm-up arena, her jaw dropping slack at the huge number of horses sharing the area. She moved to one corner and began to warm Monnie up as she had done many times before, riding large and small circles to engage her hocks, then moving onto the straight line to do a full circuit of the warm up arena to stretch her frame. That's when Monnie raised her tail high in the air and began to prance, her jerky high-knee action performed like a well-seasoned circus pony. Never having experienced this before, Aimee was unprepared for the mighty buck that followed. Suddenly she was flying through the air, feeling weightless; she heard the thunder of hooves nearby that faded off in the distance. She didn't even really feel herself hit the ground and sprawl out on the sand like a rag doll. She just knew she was no longer airborne. Then she felt the pain from the impact of landing, heard Sarah screaming as she ran towards her: "Aimee! Aimee!" Fear marred her face.

Then others were around her, the event paramedics first to arrive. She could hear them: "Wake up, honey. Come on … are you okay?"

Aimee's vision cleared as her helmet was slowly removed. A strong hand supported the back of her neck and a hand around her wrist checked her pulse.

"Monnie!" Aimee screeched, suddenly trying to rise. "Where's Monnie?"

"Here she is," a voice yelled from a distance. "She's okay."

"And you, Miss, lie still," the paramedic said, easing her back down. "Let's just check you over."

Then a distraught Sarah reached her, thanking the person who was holding Monnie as she made it through the crowd. But getting to Aimee's side was more important. Aimee could see her visually checking for injuries.

"Aimee … Aimee, are you okay?"

"Yes, I think so." Aimee tried to sit up, but felt giddy, the dizziness keeping her grounded. "I'll be okay."

"No, we are taking you to the medical post for observation. Did you hit your head?"

"I don't know, but I'll be okay to ride."

"Only if we say so," the man said firmly.

"No …" Aimee shook her head. "I must ride. It's important. Please."

"Aimee, your health is more important. There'll be other competitions," Sarah said.

"No …" Tears filled Aimee's eyes.

"Aimee," the paramedic said gently, "let's take you back to the first aid tent for a checkup, then we can assess whether you can ride or not. We don't want you to hurt yourself any further."

With that, Aimee sighed deeply. She just had to ride! "I have worked so hard for today. So has Sarah. Please don't stop me riding. I may not get another chance for a long while," she pleaded.

"Let's just keep an eye on you for a while and we'll know if you are able to ride or not. If there is no severe damage, and you feel alright …"

"But I'll miss my first event," Aimee said, a tear falling.

The ambulance arrived and Aimee was carefully placed on a stretcher and transported back to the first aid tent at the other end of the field. She was promptly attended to by the senior medical officer who prodded and poked and checked for broken bones or dislocated joints. Sarah remained by her side.

"Monnie?" Aimee asked. "Where's Monnie?"

"She's okay. She's been taken back to the float and taken care of so don't panic about her. Apparently, there was a stallion nearby and Monnie decided to show off, and you weren't expecting it. But she's okay. Karen is here and is looking after her."

Fifteen minutes later, during which Aimee rested and caught her breath, and watched the clock, the doctor came back to her.

"Well, it looks like you were just winded for a while, and apart from a few bruises that will appear in the next day or so, you have come out of it fairly lightly."

Then an official arrived at the tent. She heard him ask: "Is Aimee Gardiner capable of riding, or should we scratch her from the event?"

"No! I'm riding!" Aimee blurted out before the doctor could answer.

"Determined, aren't you, young lady," he smiled and turned back to the official. "Can you move her to the end of the list? She just needs a few more minutes."

"Oh, thank you," Aimee said, smiling broadly.

"You just lay quietly for another ten minutes and you should be right to go."

To pass the time, Aimee lay quietly. Momentarily she had

forgotten the test movements, like they had been completely knocked out of her brain. She lay, silently panicking until she visualised herself riding down the centre line, then tracking right, then … it all started coming back, and by the time the doctor came back and said, "Okay, it's showtime for you, young lady. Good luck out there and no repeat performances, okay?" she had ridden the test six times in her head.

"Okay," she said, sliding from the stretcher and feeling the bruises nagging in her thigh and shoulder. She thanked him again, gingerly waved goodbye and hurried toward the float to prepare Monnie for the big event.

This time she vowed to be ready if Monnie tried to be boss again.

With just under half an hour to go until Aimee's turn, Sarah quickly saddled Monnie while Aimee retrieved her gear and dusted off her coat, ready to climb on board. Pain shot up her arm and across her shoulder as she slid her arm into the sleeve, but she bit her lip and forced her jacket up over her back.

She mounted with Sarah's help and gave her gallant steed a stern warning. "Now do that again and I will continue working you after the test … and you'll not get any carrots tonight."

Aimee returned to the warm-up area which now was not as full as before, and there was certainly no stallion nearby to tease the mare, which Aimee felt relieved about. As if feeling guilty for what she had done, Monnie performed like a well-oiled machine, obeying every command precisely and looking like a queen in the middle of a parade.

"Keep it up, Monnie, please," Aimee whispered so no one else would hear.

Now Aimee started to feel that her left shoulder had stiffened, and sharps jabs of pain shot out now and then. She assumed it was the bruise constricted by her jacket and ignored it; kept loosening up for her test. She certainly wouldn't say anything to Sarah in case she stopped her from riding.

"Aimee Gardiner, please report to the gear checker," she heard over the loudspeaker.

Aimee quickly found the appropriate one and reported to her as requested.

"Were you the one who fell off?" the gear checker asked.

"Yes," Aimee replied. "But I'm okay now."

After checking the gear thoroughly, the checker said, "You're next up, so make your way down to the judge along the left-hand side of the arena."

Aimee gave Monnie a last reassuring pat as she did, quickly observing the final movements of the previous rider's test. Then she was acknowledged by the judge and was soon riding circles behind the A markers at the far end.

Like the sound of a starter's gun, the horn tooted, and she quickly gathered her thoughts and entered the arena at A. This was a preliminary test, and Aimee rode it accurately, ensuring her lightness in the saddle and precisely placed aids allowed Monnie to remain fluid and rhythmical beneath her. She was learning, this was all about elegance and grace, no stumbles, no flusters, no resistance. 'Don't pull,' Sarah had always told her. 'Always ride forward into her bridle as pulling creates resistance.' This stayed in her head for every transition, and every halt. 'Ride forward into her bridle.'

The test flowed well, but nevertheless, Aimee was glad when they finally halted at G. Her arm now ached, but she managed a smile on receiving a round of applause from the sidelines, that alone telling her that Monnie had done her proud – she had performed admirably.

After giving Monnie a final pat on her neck and Sarah a huge smile, Aimee made her way to the end of the arena, quickly dismounted and ran her stirrups up so they would not bang against Monnie's sides. She needed to rest her arm, and have a drink, but her name was immediately called over the PA.

"Aimee Gardiner, please report for gear-checking."

She quickly pulled her stirrups down again. "Sarah, can you help me back on?"

Sarah bunked her up. "You lost your half-hour break by riding last in the first test. Here, have a quick drink. Monnie will be okay until she gets back."

"Sarah, I haven't had time to remember the test. I always have time to see it, and watch it. What if I forget it?"

"Calm down." Sarah's hand gripped her knee. "Say to yourself … I know the test and will ride like a champion."

Aimee took a deep breath, murmured to herself, "I know the test and will ride like a champion. I know the test and will ride like a champion." She was still muttering this when she presented herself to the gear checker, the whole time watching the competitor in the arena riding turns and circles. It all started coming back.

"Your next in," the gear checker alerted her.

Aimee turned Monnie towards the judge's car and rode in that direction, trying to ignore the increasing pain developing in her shoulder.

"Aimee, are you okay?" the judge asked in a concerned voice.

"Yes, fine thank you," she lied, trying to breathe through the increasing pain and the light-headed feeling washing over her face. Then she was heading down to the A end, and receiving the now-familiar sound of the horn.

She entered at A, halted confidently at X, barely smiling. On the judge's returning salute, Aimee continued her test, her thoughts becoming fuzzy as overwhelming pain blanketed her shoulder. She pushed Monnie into a nice working trot and began to turn left when suddenly the judge's horn blew.

Aimee froze and she immediately realised that she'd gone the wrong way. That was going to cost her in points. Quickly composing herself, she blocked out the pain and continued, finishing an otherwise accurate test of sharper corners and smaller circles that required riding stronger. But the stronger she rode, the greater the pain that shot through her shoulder. Monnie must have sensed it as, partway through the movement, she seemed to take over, performing the remainder of the test as if she was on automatic. She finished the test with a beautiful square halt, all four feet firmly planted beneath her. Aimee was extremely grateful as she knew that might have made up for those lost points from her error.

The pain now almost unbearable, Aimee's eyes clouded with tears as she left the arena. Sarah quickly ran to her, catching her as she slid down and crumpled on the ground, holding her left arm and complaining of the pain.

Then Karen appeared beside Sarah and grabbed Monnie's reins, allowing Sarah to attend to Aimee properly and moving Monnie out of the way. At the same time, the paramedics arrived.

"I'll take Monnie back to the float?" Karen said from behind.

"Oh, please. Thank you," she replied.

Aimee was immediately lifted onto a stretcher and returned to the first aid tent.

"I wondered if I'd be seeing you again, Miss Gardiner," came the familiar voice. "Where does it hurt?"

"The back and top of my shoulder hurts," Aimee cried.

"Well, my lady, you are incredibly brave, because looking at you now, it seems you may have damaged it after all. That will mean you will have to do a trip to the hospital for x-rays. I take it you are happy to finish riding for the day?" He looked at her with a raised eyebrow.

"I guess so," Aimee muttered. She noticed the concern on Sarah's face. "I'm sorry, Sarah."

"It's alright, honey. We'll get you up the hospital and get it sorted." She half smiled, and Aimee realised there were other things on her mind too. Then it hit her – how would Monnie and all the gear get home from the show if Sarah took her to the hospital?

Her school friend, Susan, appeared at the tent opening as Aimee posed the question. "How is Monnie going to get home? You'll have to take her home first, Sarah."

Sarah squeezed her hand. "You let me worry about the details, sweetie."

Then Susan was beside them. "Hi, Aimee. Have you heard the results?"

"No."

"You came fifth in the Preliminary. Congratulations," Susan continued. "Would you like me to collect your prize for you, as I don't think you would like to do any walking at the moment."

"Yes, please. You can give it to me at school on Wednesday?" Aimee continued. Although overjoyed at the results, she felt disappointed at not being able to collect the prize herself, but also appreciated that she didn't have to move from her comfortable position. "How did you go with your preliminary?"

"I came third in the 1D," Susan replied.

"That's fantastic." Aimee gave her a big smile. "You should be really pleased with that."

Then Susan's mother arrived to collect Susan.

"Aimee, this is my mother, Liz," she introduced politely.

"Hello," Aimee responded. "And this is Sarah who looks after me."

"Congratulations, Aimee," replied Liz, smiling. "Both of you have done very well. Sarah, you must be proud of Aimee?

"I am, exceptionally so. She has worked very hard for this day. I saw Susan ride her test and she certainly deserves her prize. Well done, Susan."

"Aimee, what have you done to your shoulder?" Susan asked

as a sling was applied to immobilise the area.

"They think I might have slight dislocation, or fracture. Sarah is taking me to the hospital to have it x-rayed … after we take Monnie home," Aimee insisted strongly, but Sarah shook her head.

"We don't live far from you and have a space on our float," Liz cut in. "We could take your horse home for you, Sarah, so you can take Aimee straight away. Just tell us where you would like her put."

Relief washed over Sarah's face. "Oh, thank you so much." She breathed a heavy sigh. "If Aimee can wait here, I will go and pack all the gear away in the car and get Monnie for you … she floats very well," she added as she ducked out of the tent and headed to the car. "I'll be back with the car to pick you up, Aimee," she said, her voice fading.

So, to hospital it was. X-rays were taken, painkillers administered and strict instructions delivered that she was not to ride until cleared by her doctor.

They arrived home to Karen's warm welcome and were informed that Monnie had arrived safely and had been bedded down and rugged, and all the horses were likewise. Aimee suddenly realised what a close-knit fraternity the horsy set were, all pitching in to help out when things went wrong.

Gingerly, she hugged Sarah goodnight and ended a very eventful day. While she had sampled only a portion of her dream, she knew it would be a while before she would get any closer.

Chapter 9

Time to Bounce Back

Aimee returned to school on the Wednesday, looking forward to collecting her ribbon and the results of her test. She found Susan sitting outside the classroom and asked the results of the Novice test.

"I got fourth in the Preliminary and third in the Novice," Susan blurted out, showing Aimee her ribbons.

"Oh, Susan, that's fantastic. You should be very happy with that," Aimee gushed, waiting for Susan to tell her the rest of the results. But Susan didn't say anything about Aimee's tests and Aimee wondered whether she didn't want to break the bad news to her. But, after a minute, Susan reached into her bag and retrieved a third ribbon and a fifth ribbon, along with Aimee's test results.

"Congratulations, Aimee. That is amazing considering the amount of pain you were in. You had some real competition in your class so what you achieved is fabulous."

"I guess so." Aimee huffed, her disappointment at not gaining a higher place obvious. Only the first two place-getters would be selected for the National team.

"Hey, don't be disappointed. There'll be other opportunities," Susan consoled, to which Aimee shrugged.

Then the school siren blasted out its raucous warning to be in class, and the girls hurried off.

Later that day, Aimee visited her mother to tell her the news of the weekend. When they arrived at the hospital, Aimee and Sarah were informed that Rachael's condition had improved and she'd been moved to an independent living wing where she would be encouraged to be more self-reliant, an intern explaining the benefits of time and reassuring them this was a positive move. With a map of the hospital being turned this way and that, they eventually found the appropriate wing, and the right room.

Rachael was reading a book in her self-contained unit when they knocked and entered.

"Hello, sweetheart," Rachael said, giving Aimee a hug.

"Hi, Mum. How are feeling? You look so much better. Are you managing on your own now?"

"I am, and I am feeling more and more ready to come home again. I've not had a drink for so long now and I feel like I don't want to drink anymore. That's a good sign, isn't it?"

Aimee knew she should feel elated, that her mother, after all this time, was finally getting better. Her life would soon return to normal. But she also felt downhearted at the thought of leaving Sarah's, and instantly wondered when things returned to normal if she might not be able to pursue her dreams as far as she would like to. But her mother was … had to be her priority.

"That's great, Mum. How soon do you think you will be home?"

"Well, they say they would like me to stay here for a while. We are aiming for me to be home for your birthday so we can celebrate it together, sweetheart." Then Rachael turned to Sarah. "Thank you for looking after Aimee but I think it's important I come home soon. I am missing out on seeing her grow, seeing her achievements and *I* need to be responsible for her care."

Sarah's lips thinned and she looked momentarily out the window, then nodded in agreeance. She glanced at Aimee, and half smiled her assurance that all would be fine.

Her birthday was two months away, Aimee realised, and she and Sarah had planned for her to compete in the State Indoor Dressage Championships. A win at the championships would earn her enough points to compete at Elementary level and then aim at Medium level. Aimee was still learning the more difficult movements which meant she had to work Monnie consistently to build the muscles to achieve it.

"I look forward to that," she said with all the honesty she could muster, "but do you feel you'll be able to manage everything at home?" Aimee asked.

"Well, that's why I'm here now, isn't it. It's designed to help me slide back into a normal lifestyle where I am able to look after myself without the aid of … of … you know. This time I really do want to help myself and look after you properly. I don't ever want to let you down again."

Aimee had heard this so many times before, but never from a sober mum.

Sarah stood in the background, looking slightly drawn.

"Will I still be able to compete with Sarah when you come home?" Aimee asked warily. She couldn't stop the question coming out of her mouth. "I've got the State Indoor Championships coming up soon and I don't want to miss them."

"Sure, you can go, and you will still be able to ride on weekends, just like you've always done."

Now Aimee felt slightly more excited at the concept of having her mother home, but deep down she also wondered how much her lifestyle would change. An hour later, Aimee made excuses to leave – she had homework to do for the next day. Saying goodnight to her mum, she and Sarah left for Trailblazers, detouring via a fast food outlet on the way home. As they waited for the order, Sarah slipped her arm around Aimee's shoulder. "I am going to miss doing this," she said openly. "It's been sort of great having you around."

Those words stayed with Aimee through the night. They had been together for ten months and she would sure miss Sarah too.

Chapter 10

An Even Bigger Challenge

Soon enough, the State Championships date arrived and Aimee felt fully prepared for the new quest.

She was now more experienced; knew exactly how she would ride each test. After many pep talks with Monnie, they were now a formidable team and well known for their desire to win. Having ridden her for so long, it was almost like Monnie was hers, they had become like one.

The trip into the showgrounds was also a routine journey, and Aimee felt so familiar with the procedures of these competitions she enjoyed the environment immensely. With the memories of that one disastrous competition still fresh in her mind, she now stayed more mentally alert during her warm ups. She certainly didn't want a repeat performance, even though Monnie had been exemplary at all the shows they'd attended since that fateful day.

Then came the familiar sound of her name being called over the PA: Report to the gear checkers.

"Good luck," said the gear checker as Aimee rode off towards the judge's car parked at the C end.

Aimee began her first competitive Elementary test, quickly realising it was a lot harder than she'd expected. The movements seemed shorter but quicker than in practice, the arena seemed smaller, but the test still flowed well and Monnie coped with it well. Although Aimee felt pleased at achieving her short-term goal of reaching another level, she still had higher accolades and dreams to fulfil.

She completed the Elementary test with no mistakes and what she considered a reasonably accurate test. The other competitors also rode exceptionally well and she knew her test would have to have been brilliant to achieve any of the higher places. She also felt confident though that she was in the vicinity.

She did not dare take the leap into the next level of Medium – it was out of her league at the moment. But not for long, she hoped.

Sarah greeted Aimee at the end of the arena, excited at her performance. "Well done, darling. That was fantastic. You must be very pleased."

"It wasn't as polished as I would have liked, but I'm happy with the way Monnie went," Aimee replied as they returned to the stables to unsaddle and pack the gear in the car ready for the journey home. Then they returned to the grandstand to watch the more advanced riders perform some of the higher tests. To Aimee, it was like watching magic, the magic of silent communication between horse and rider. Sarah commentated softly from beside her as to what movement went well and what a rider did wrong when a movement was less than perfect. This alone was a great teaching tool, watching others excel or fail.

Between tests, Aimee suddenly heard her name over the PA again. Her jaw dropped open. She had placed third in her test and was requested to go to the score room to collect her prize. Sarah clasped her in a bear hug, which seemed to go on forever.

Keeping up traditions, they celebrated with the traditional block of chocolate on the drive home.

Chapter 11

An Unexpected Worry

Aimee woke the following morning to the familiar sound of the phone, which didn't usually ring this early. *Nobody rings before 7am,* Aimee thought briefly. She assumed Sarah must have answered it and turned over into her pillow.

"Aimee," Sarah shouted. "It's your mum on the phone."

Quickly, Aimee swung out of bed and ran down the hall, wondering why she was calling so early. She suddenly realised this might be the moment she'd been dreading. It might be the day she had to return home. She picked up the phone, only to see the teary look in Sarah's eyes.

"Good morning, Mum," she replied hesitantly. "How are you?"

"Great," Rachael replied. "I am coming home today. I'm well again, and I am looking forward to having you with me. We can both continue our lives again."

"Sure, Mum. That will be fantastic," Aimee cried, now feeling emotionally shredded.

"So, will you come home after school today?" Rachael asked. "I'm sure Sarah will help you pack."

"I'll talk to Sarah. I haven't been home for a while, so I'm not sure what condition the house is in," Aimee worried.

"That's okay. We will be able to make it home again together. Alright, I will see you after school, my darling. Bye for now."

Aimee replaced the receiver on the hook and froze with

numbness. She had not prepared herself for this day to arrive so soon. She turned to Sarah, a tear in her eye, and fell into Sarah's outstretched arms.

Sarah hugged her. "Everything will work out for you, Aimee. I will be here to help you fulfil your dreams. We will do it, Aimee, I promise," Sarah cried.

They finished breakfast in silence until Aimee announced that she had better get ready for school. Slowly, she retreated to her bedroom and packed her school bag with her books and a small photo album of her achievements that Sarah had been collecting over the past year.

Aimee quickly forgot that it was her birthday the next day.

Chapter 12

The Beauty of Friends

Arriving at school, Aimee suddenly realised she needed to talk to Susan, as a friend. Dabbling around the edges of her issues, she told her about the third place she'd received then that she had to return home to her mother that afternoon. She felt strange confiding in Susan as she'd never before needed to analyse such a complicated problem.

Susan listened calmly, her concern evident. "I'm so sorry, Aimee," she said after Aimee told her story. "I had no idea. But surely you can still ride Monnie regularly."

Aimee shook her head. "It's quite a ride to Trailblazers. I can't see how I can during the week and still get home before dark."

"I'm sure we can work out some way that your mum will let you. We just have to think up an excuse that you have to go there." She gripped her arm. "You think about it, and I'll think about it, and between us we'll soon fudge an excuse that your mother will have to let you go."

For the first time in Aimee's life, she felt she was dishonest drumming up lame excuses to ensure she could go to Sarah's during the week, but she also knew it might be a necessity if she was to achieve her dreams.

The final bell went earlier than expected, and Aimee ambled down to the car park to meet Sarah. To her surprise, Sarah was immersed in conversation with Rachael, who appeared more contented with life than she'd ever been.

"Hello, darling," Rachael said. "How was school?"

Sarah remained quiet and gave Aimee a reassuring smile.

"Sarah and I have both agreed that we would like to take you out to dinner tonight. Your choice," Rachael added.

"Great. Could we go to that little Italian restaurant downtown? I really feel like some lasagna tonight."

Sarah and Rachael agreed.

"We'll follow Sarah back to her place for you to collect your things and we'll go to dinner from there. How does that sound?" Rachael said, taking control.

"Mum, can I go and feed Monnie first and say goodbye and explain to her that I won't be there for her in the morning."

Rachael frowned that Aimee considered a horse capable of understanding. "Okay, if that's what you want," she agreed.

"Mum, you could meet Monnie if you like. She is the sweetest horse ever," Aimee said.

"That would be nice. I guess I will have to get used to this affiliation with horses, won't I?" Rachael mused aloud.

Sarah and Aimee glanced at each other as if Rachael had spoken a different language.

They arrived at Sarah's where Rachael clearly looked and felt like a foreigner, but she tried hard to appear enthusiastic; she had even stopped in the driveway and spent a long moment scrutinizing the Trailblazer's sign before continuing on down the driveway and parking the car.

"Mum, this is Monnie. She's Sarah's competition horse. But I have been riding her for Sarah. We are now doing Elementary dressage and hoping to be doing Medium by the end of the year," Aimee gushed after leading her mother down to the paddocks.

"Oh, well done," said Rachael. "Elementary. Is that the basic level?" Rachael clarified innocently.

"No," said Aimee smiling, and then went on to explain the various levels of dressage and what was needed to achieve each new level.

The rest of the visit clearly showed Rachael did not share Aimee's passion. Aimee understood her mother's feelings, but continued the tour anyway.

When Sarah returned from feeding the horses, she continued the conversation with Rachael while Aimee tended to Monnie. "Aimee is a very talented and dedicated horse rider, Rachael. I am still very keen to support her, but I can only do it with your support and acceptance."

"She has certainly taken to you, Sarah," Rachael scowled.

Sarah's eyebrow rose at the comment and tone. "We're like sisters," she said, trying to smile, "and I really do want to help Aimee achieve her dreams." Then excusing herself, she turned and went back to the house to get ready for dinner. Aimee gathered her things in preparation for the next episode of her entangled life, Rachael assisting Aimee in packing the car. On noticing the box of newly acquired trophies and ribbons, she looked up proudly at her daughter.

At the local Italian restaurant, they were surprised at the amount of food placed in front of them and knew they would not be hungry for a long time.

"Aimee, I want to give you this in case I don't see you tomorrow," Sarah said as she passed Aimee her birthday present.

Aimee's eyes lit up, remembering how Sarah had spoilt her last year.

"Oh, thank you, Sarah," and Aimee leapt up and gave Sarah one of her enormous hugs, even before she had opened it.

"It is beautiful. Please put it on me, Sarah," Aimee said as she admired her new gold watch with a horse head in the middle.

Sarah fastened the new watch on Aimee's wrist, smiling at Aimee's excitement.

"I've never had a watch before," she told her, turning her wrist to admire it further. "It makes me feel grown up."

The conversation continued throughout the meal, the main topic remaining on Aimee's achievements and her future goals, Aimee keeping her mother involved so she didn't feel an outsider, her mother consciously making an effort to keep up with the conversation to be accepted.

As the night moved on and everybody had an early start, Sarah drove Rachael and Aimee back to Trailblazers to collect their car.

"It's going to be lonely without you," Sarah admitted when she and Aimee were alone, her thoughts tumbling out unintentionally. "It's been nice having you around."

Then Rachael appeared beside them.

"And if you'd like to ride Monnie during the week, I could collect you from school," Sarah offered, which immediately solved Aimee's dilemma.

But Rachael quickly interjected. "I am sure we can come to some arrangement. I will be in touch."

On that departing note, Aimee began to feel uncomfortable with the new arrangement.

Chapter 13

The Bonding Moment

Over the next few weeks, Rachael and Aimee talked and reminisced, trying to find a bonding moment, but Aimee's mind was always on Sarah and Monnie. She continued her weekend riding, but Rachael wouldn't allow her to ride during the week. To compensate, Aimee studied more to fill the void.

Rachael's health continued to improve and she no longer depended on Aimee for her survival. She had also secured a part-time job at the local primary school. Occasionally, she watched Aimee ride at Trailblazers, but without the same enthusiasm Sarah had. Aimee noted this was a huge improvement on her previous role as a mother, and gradually accepted this as part of her life but would not let it interfere with her dreams.

Eventually, she had convinced her mother of the importance of working Monnie more regularly if she was to succeed at the level she was now riding, and, although Rachael had made it clear she did not want to relinquish her time with Aimee, she also realised the importance of her request.

"How was your lesson, sweetheart?" Rachael asked as Aimee bounced through the door one afternoon.

"Great! We worked on flying changes today. Oh, let me explain … they are when you ask the horse to change canter leads whilst in the air so that you have a different leading canter leg when they take the next stride."

"Oh, that's nice. Is it hard to ride?"

"To teach Monnie to do it is hard, but once she got the hang of it, she was fine. It's now a matter of me staying balanced when I ask her."

With that, they both sat down to dinner, where the conversation mainly revolved around school and her mum's new job. Aimee was grateful that her life was now at least normal, and she could plan a routine again.

As the night crept on, Aimee excused herself to study for a human biology test the following day. Her mum kissed her goodnight, knowing she would not see her again before she went to bed.

The next morning, they both rose early to complete all the chores before going off to their prospective schools. As Rachael did not start till nine o'clock, she could take Aimee to school in the mornings. That morning, Aimee noticed her mother was not as coherent as usual and wondered whether she had picked up a virus overnight.

"Mum, are you okay? You look a bit washed out this morning."

Rachael snapped back. "Yes, of course I am."

It was now Friday, and Aimee's excitement grew at the prospect of riding for two days and competing at the local pony club dressage championship where she would be in an elite field doing the Elementary test. It was her big chance to cement her name in the dressage circle as she was still riding as a junior. Her other big wish was that her mother would watch her ride and more fully understand her passion and desire.

"Mum, please, will you come and watch me on Sunday? I would love to have you there. Please …" she continued.

"I would love to, darling, but I just have so much to do around here, and I really feel I need to do it," Rachael replied sulkily.

Aimee sighed with deep disappointment. "That's okay, Mum." She finished her dinner then went into the kitchen to help with the dishes as she wanted to be at Sarah's early in the morning to prepare Monnie for Sunday.

Sarah was delighted to see Aimee and greeted her with the usual big hug and enormous smile. "How are you going? How is your mum? Is everything okay?"

Aimee didn't want to say anything about what she'd noticed as she hoped it was just a virus and nothing more.

The morning lesson went especially well. Monnie performed all the required movements exceptionally well, which boosted Aimee's enthusiasm about the competition. She just prayed she'd be able to reproduce that same quality the next day. Then she took Monnie over to the wash bay and gave her a bath and trim so she looked spectacular on the day. The rest of the day was filled with packing the car and helping out with the usual chores. Saturday night arrived quicker than expected, and Rachael had agreed to let Aimee stay at Sarah's for the night as they had an early start the next morning, and Aimee needed to be with Monnie.

Aimee had now competed at so many shows that the entry procedure was so routine and everything had become automatic. She arrived at the gear checker without her name being called as she had watched the previous competitor. Then, as always, she made her way to the judge in preparation for the test. As this was now her fourth Elementary test, the arena did not appear to be so small, and she maneuvered Monnie around it more easily.

After a wonderfully accurate test, she halted at G and saluted, which indicated to the judge she had completed her test. This brought the familiar beaming smile to both Aimee's and Sarah's faces. Aimee knew she'd done well this time and looked forward to hearing the results after they had been calculated.

"Sarah, I feel like I'm ready for the Medium test now. Do you think I can attempt one at the next show?" Aimee asked.

This was a question Sarah had been waiting for and had already prepared the answer. "Let's try some of the movements next week and see how well you and Monnie cope with them, shall we?" Sarah replied.

With that, they returned to the float and prepared Monnie for the return trip home, and a well-rested afternoon.

"Ladies and Gentlemen, we have the results of the Elementary test. In first place is Aimee Gardiner on Monique." Sarah and Aimee hugged and jumped so high they did not hear the names of the other placegetters. But it didn't matter.

They both hurried to the clubhouse to collect Aimee's ribbon and to check her score. As they stood reading over the judge's comments, they were approached by one of the top riders in the state.

"Are you Aimee Gardiner?" she asked.

"Yes. Yes, I am," Aimee said.

"My name is Hillary Summers, and I would like to invite you to try out for the state junior dressage squad."

Aimee felt suddenly numb – she had never considered this avenue so early in her career, but immediately realised the importance of the opportunity.

"She would like that very much," Sarah cut in quickly. "Tell the nice lady, Aimee," Sarah prompted as Aimee stood with her mouth wide open.

"I … I would like that very much. Thank you so much," Aimee gushed, her grin spreading enormously.

They discussed the logistics of being a squad member and the obligations expected from her, Aimee all the while figeting with the ribbon, which now seemed so insignificant compared to what she had just been offered.

Aimee and Sarah returned home in time to put everything

away and Monnie to bed before Rachael arrived to collect her for the week.

"Mum … Mum, guess what?" Aimee blurted out as she ran towards her mother. "I've been asked to join the state dressage squad. Isn't that fantastic!"

Rachael half-smiled. "I guess that will mean more time needed here at Sarah's." She drew a deep breath, then forced the smile wider. "That is wonderful. When do you start, and by the way, how did you go today?"

"I came first! I wish you had been there. Monnie went so well."

"Are you ready to come home now?" Rachael asked. "You can tell me all about it when we get home."

The trip home was Aimee's moment of glory: she had finally achieved another part of her dream by conquering yet another level of dressage and had been selected for the state squad. She now had endless opportunities, including lessons from some of the top coaches in the state.

Rachael picked up Chinese takeaway on the way home, and they sat down to a most enjoyable meal. They talked about the day, and Aimee blurted out that she'd been recognised by the best. She didn't notice her mother's eyes harden or hear the deep intake of her breath. Then her mother looked up and smiled at her and Aimee thought that everything was absolutely perfect.

At school the following day, Susan promptly greeted Aimee.

"I didn't see you at the show yesterday," Aimee said.

"No. Mum and Dad had to work so they couldn't take me."

"Oh, I wish you had told me because I'm sure we could have picked you up," Aimee responded. "Please, if that ever happens again, let me know and I can ask Sarah if she wouldn't mind taking you."

"Thank you so much. Mum and Dad have to work on

weekends regularly which makes it difficult to get out, so I am very grateful when they can take me."

Given Susan's disappointment, Aimee didn't feel it appropriate to tell her about her squad offer in case she became jealous – she didn't want to upset their friendship, as this friendship with Susan was growing stronger.

Chapter 14

Growing Friendships

Aimee returned home from school grateful for a day off from riding as she still felt tired from the excitement of the competition. Monnie needed a rest too, as she had also worked exceptionally hard.

Her mother had not yet arrived home from school, which Aimee considered unusual. Nevertheless, she decided to surprise her mother by having dinner prepared for when she arrived. Rummaging through the freezer, she found some chicken with which she could make a chicken curry – her favourite quick meal. Having put the chicken and ingredients together, she put the water on to boil the rice, still waiting anxiously for her mother's return. She was now over an hour late, and her mum didn't carry a mobile, so she couldn't contact her.

Aimee started to pace the kitchen floor. She also had no idea where her mother could be. Then she saw a car's headlights shine into the driveway; heard the clunk of a car door closing then the opening of the front door.

"Hi, Mum. I've cooked your favourite dinner," she said, trying to throw off the worry. "I hope you enjoy it."

"Thank you, sweetheart. You are a gem," Rachael replied.

"You're late tonight. I was getting worried. You didn't say you were going to be late."

"I went to see my counsellor today. She wanted to know how I was going."

"Was she happy with your progress?"

"Oh yes. There are still some things I need to resolve, but overall she is happy with me."

"Mum, do you want to talk to me about them? Maybe I can help."

"Not tonight, darling. I feel a bit drained at the moment. Maybe tomorrow, if you don't mind."

Aimee suddenly felt empty, and frowned that maybe things weren't as normal as she'd hoped.

They ate in silence then both retired early, Aimee tossing and turning for most of the night.

Aimee's mum was already at the breakfast table when she arrived in the kitchen.

"Mum, do you want to talk about your issues now?" Aimee asked, aware that time was against her.

"How about we go out tonight and talk about it over dinner," Rachael suggested. "We both have to be at school soon. And sweetheart, please don't be alarmed. I just have some adjusting to do, that's all."

They finished breakfast and headed off to their respective schools.

The afternoon arrived quickly, and Rachael greeted Aimee at the school gate as usual, and they headed home.

Rachael pottered about making Aimee something for afternoon tea – a cup of Milo with cake – all the while Aimee wanted to reignite the discussion that had stalled that morning. Her concern had been growing that whatever was troubling her mother would disrupt her sort of 'normal' life.

Rachael eased herself into a chair across from Aimee and heaved a deep sigh. "Aimee, I think I am ready to tell you what has been troubling me now," she began.

Aimee breathed a slight sigh of relief. They could work on her mother's issues together.

"Darling, I am finding it hard to accept the amount of time you are spending with the horses. I really feel that you don't want to be with me anymore."

"Oh, Mum. I am so sorry!" Blood rushed to Aimee's face and her heart started to pound. This was not what she'd expected. Unsure of what to say next, her mouth opened and closed several times as she tried to drum up words that would not offend her mother and destroy their newfound friendship. "Mum, I wish so much for you to be a part of my passion. I want to be able to have both you and my riding equally. Can you please try to understand … all my life I have had this burning need to be a dressage rider – a very successful dressage rider – but I don't want to lose your love and friendship." Aimee's tears began to fall. What was her mother asking of her?

Rachael rose and moved around the table, and wrapped her arms around Aimee. "But I feel like I'm intruding when you and Sarah are together. Sarah knows so much and is so willing to help you, where I don't seem to be able to be of any use to you at all." Aimee could hear the pain in her voice.

"Mum, you are so wrong. Sarah will never be able to replace you. But please understand, I really need to do this – I really want this to be my life, but I have to establish a name now or I'll be overlooked. All the top names started young, and they now have lots of people training under them. That's what I want to do. Please understand, and I really need your support in this."

Tears rolling down her cheeks, her eyes pleading, Aimee looked up at her mother. "There's so much you could do to be a part of this, and help us. You don't even have to go near the horses if you don't want to. Just for you to be there would be a dream come true. It would give you an interest, instead of just sitting at home."

"But, Aimee, what does Sarah think of me being so illiterate when it comes to the horse side of things?" Rachael quipped back.

"Mum, Sarah had to start from somewhere, and you can do the same. Please, Mum, I would love to have you just come down and watch me. I want to make you proud and give you something to want to live for."

Silence fell between them, with no solution or compromise forthcoming. Then her mother said, "Come on, we'd better eat this beautiful left-over curry of yours."

Over dinner, the conversation continued, Aimee pushing her curry around the plate while her mother sat staring at her chicken on its bed of freshly fried rice. Neither meal posed any answers.

"Mum," Aimee finally piped up, "will you just talk to Sarah and let her know how you're feeling."

She kept her eyes on her plate, feeling the need to fight for her dreams but not wanting to see the disappointment on her mother's face. She felt again that she had to be so much older than her age to get her mother to see reason. She pushed the point further, pushed a ball of curry harder across the plate. "I need Sarah. She is helping me take this where I want it to go. She is giving me all the chances to be somebody, to be what I want to be." *There it's out!* She half looked up to view her mother's expression and started to feel insecure again.

"You must realise, Aimee, that I am so jealous of what you and Sarah have between you. We have never had, and can never have, a friendship like you two have. I am your mother! And you never told me before how important this riding thing is to you."

Aimee fixed her gaze on the table. "It's me, Mum. All I can ever think about is how far I can take this. I'm good at it, and I like the way I feel when I compete. I'd like you to be a part of it."

Her mother let out a big sigh and shook her head, accepting defeat. "Okay, so when are you riding next?"

"Tomorrow, if that's okay, Mum."

"Okay. So, I will pick you up from school tomorrow and we will go straight to Sarah's, and I will watch you ride. How does that sound?" Rachael's eyes twinkled when Aimee looked up from the table, a broad smile spreading across her face. "… and I will also try and talk to Sarah about how I feel so that we can make this dream of yours come true."

Aimee leapt up and hugged her mother enormously. "Thank you … thank you, thank you, thank you. I will make you proud of me."

"I am proud of you, my beautiful girl. I always have been."

They picked up their forks and enjoyed the rest of their meal, feeling closer to each other than they had ever been.

Chapter 15

Trying Times

The following afternoon, Aimee wondered if her mother would keep her promise, and was elated to find her waiting for her in the school car park as promised. She chatted away on the way to Trailblazers, and felt only a little apprehensive spending her afternoon with her mother and Sarah together. It was like her two separate worlds were colliding together.

Monnie was already saddled and waiting for Aimee when they arrived, and Aimee quickly headed for the house to change into riding clothes. She was soon mounted, after giving Rachael a polite introduction to her best four-legged friend in the world. Then she headed into the arena to warm Monnie up, riding stretching exercises of circles and straight lines, and flexing exercises on either rein. After fifteen minutes, Aimee concentrated on some difficult dressage movements, conscious of the conversation going on between Sarah and her mum. Although there was no animosity apparent, Aimee worried about how insecure her mother felt in Sarah's presence.

After an hour, Monnie had worked well enough and Aimee began to cool her down with lighter exercises that would prevent her muscles from tightening. After ten minutes, she headed back to the stables, followed by Rachael and Sarah, and began to unsaddle Monnie to prepare her for her stable and night feed.

"What can I do to help?" Rachael asked keenly, waiting for a response.

Sarah already had the reins as Aimee undid the girth and removed the saddle.

"Here, Mum. Can you take the saddle and I'll show you how to put it into its cover, which is on the rail behind you."

Rachael picked up the vinyl saddle cover and tried to work out how to fit it over the saddle. Then Aimee showed her the correct way, which then made sense, her smile more important to Aimee than the fact she actually managed to do it without dropping the saddle. Sarah had led Monnie away to the wash bay to hose off the sweat she had built up, leaving Aimee and Rachael to make up Monnie's night feed. Then Sarah led Monnie into her stall and showed Rachael how to fit her rug. Aimee's heart swelled to see them working together, and chatting, and hoped this would become the normal way of life.

"You were great, Mum," Aimee gushed as they headed for the house for a well-earned cup of tea. Yet she glanced behind her to Sarah, aware of her friend's quietness that day. Could she also be feeling put out by her mother's presence?

Over a brew, they discussed the upcoming competitions and how it was important for Aimee's career, especially now that she'd been accepted as a squad member of the state team.

"And what will my role be in all this?" Rachael asked suddenly. "I don't want to be excluded even though I don't know much yet."

"Mum, your role is very important," Aimee assured her. "You are responsible for the refreshments; you're the cheer squad and the moral support." Rachael nodded.

"Yes, I can be all those things. But I can be even more."

When Rachael and Aimee said goodnight and made their way home, Sarah stood watching them drive away down the road then returned to her cold, lonely house that had lost its ray of sunshine. Even so, she felt pleased that Aimee's mother was clearly making a concerted effort to support her daughter.

Chapter 16

More Dilemma

Aimee rested her cheeks on her knuckles as her eyes scanned the page in front of her. It seemed her homework had doubled and she had to cram much longer to pass the seemingly endless flow of tests inflicted on Year 12s. With homework and exam study, she had to become more proficient at time management, or she would never get out of her room. That thought made her feel guilty that her mother was left to occupy her own time.

Footsteps sounded in the hall. "Just me, sweetheart. I thought you'd need some sustenance." Her mother appeared in the doorway with a much-needed cup of Milo. "… and maybe take a little time out to rest your brain."

"Thanks, Mum. But I really have to finish this so I can spend some time with you."

Her mum was looking so well these days, which made Aimee feel even more guilty. Between training for the state squad and school commitments, she hadn't been the devoted daughter her mother needed, and she feared this would have repercussions.

"Just take regular breaks, love. You put too much pressure on yourself. I can wait until you are finished. Your schoolwork is important."

"So are you," Aimee assured her. "You are more important." She wondered if her mother understood that.

The morning sun on her face came too soon, making her

squint as she glanced at the clock on her desk. *Only five hours sleep!* Completing her homework so she could be free for the whole weekend to enjoy the horses had been a priority, but now she found it hard to raise her head from the pillow. After lying for a short while to wake fully, she rose and trudged her way to the shower, noticing her mother was still in bed, still deep in sleep. She frowned. Her mother, since recovering, was always the first to rise in the morning.

Aimee tip-toed into her room and bent over to give her mother her usual morning kiss but reeled back at the pungent smell that lingered on her mother's breath. She froze, suddenly fearful, a flood of memories of previous years tumbling in.

"Mum, wake up! Mum, please wake up!" Aimee screamed. Madly, she shook her mother from side to side, grabbed her shoulders and shook her harder.

Reluctantly, Rachael opened her eyes, groaned and pulled the covers over her head.

"Mum! Please!" Aimee continued to shake her, but without luck. She rushed to the kitchen, made a strong cup of black coffee, hoping it would bring her mother around enough to explain her actions. By the time she returned to the bedroom, Rachael had opened her eyes, her senses stirring enough to comprehend the morning.

"Mum, drink this!" Aimee barked, thrusting the coffee into Rachael's hand. "Did you drink anything last night?" She stiffened, waiting for an answer.

"I just had a few," Rachael muttered.

Aimee felt herself starting to shake. "Why, Mum? You promised you wouldn't do this again!"

"I'm sorry. I got a bit lonely, and you were so busy last night." Rachael's eyes blurred with tears.

"Does this mean we are back to square one again? Do I have to go through this hell all over again? What were you thinking?

You were doing so well!" Aimee's words fell from her mouth quicker than her mother could comprehend.

"I thought that all the talking we've done over the past weeks had resolved the issues … that you were okay with everything …"

Aimee couldn't believe it. Things *had* been going so well. Inwardly she could feel her rage rising, pushed down by the fearful thoughts of what came next. Her mother's eyes welled with tears. "Where do we go from here now, Mum?" Aimee asked, trying to keep the disappointment and anger from her voice.

"It will be okay. It was only one time. I'll be fine. I have control over the situation, darling. Please trust me."

Rachael sipped her coffee till it was empty, then staggered out of bed. Shakily, she showered and dressed then entered the kitchen where Aimee had prepared a wholesome breakfast, hoping it would restore her mother back to health. Aimee, however, felt too sick in the stomach to eat and settled for a glass of milk.

As she watched her mother eating, her thoughts turned to the weekend. All the excitement of riding for the whole weekend was gone – after this setback, she wasn't sure if she could leave her mother alone. Sadly, she contacted Sarah and told her that she might not be there that day as her mother needed her to do something for her.

The morning drifted away while grocery shopping, and in the afternoon, they played board games, Aimee mechanically pushing her token around the board. This was not the exciting weekend she had envisaged, but she knew it was necessary under the circumstances.

At one point, Rachael looked across the board game at her and said, "I'm sorry, sweetheart. Maybe you can ride Monnie tomorrow. I'll come along and watch, then we can go to a movie or something."

But this meant Aimee could only spend half a day with Sarah, not the usual full day, and she would not be there to help out. But it was better than nothing, she guessed.

The following morning, Aimee saddled Monnie quietly and spent considerable time just walking around the perimeter of the paddock, thus avoiding a lesson she felt she hadn't earned.

Finishing her workload, Sarah wandered across and leant on the railing near where Rachael sat beneath a tree.

"Hi, Rachael," she said, her gaze firmly glued to Aimee. "How are you going?"

"Oh, we are fine," Rachael replied, not wanting to let Sarah know what had happened at home.

"Has Aimee had a busy week at school? Is she okay? She missed riding yesterday."

"Oh, yes, she was just *very* tired yesterday, and I felt she needed some time at home," Rachael lied.

Dubiously, Sarah nodded. Something in Aimee's posture showed things were not as they should be. She looked deflated.

"We will need to start discussing the schedule for next week as Aimee has to attend a squad training clinic with Monnie. Are you able to come and watch?"

Reluctantly, Rachael nodded.

Shortly after, Aimee returned with Monnie. "My head is so full of exams at the moment, I just couldn't concentrate on a lesson," she explained to Sarah. "I just needed some quiet time to settle my head down."

"That's okay, sweetie. Riding laps is good for that too."

Rachael just nodded, and together they put Monnie back in the paddock.

Chapter 17

The Beginning of the Future

The school week began as it had done for the past twelve years, but Aimee knew school was coming to an end. Final exams were approaching fast. Although a confident student, she realised the added problem of dealing with her mother's deteriorating mental condition constantly distracted her thoughts. She also had concerns about her employment options for the coming year. Soon she would have to start filling out job applications, and writing resumes and trying to fit it all in around being there for her mother. But how could she get a job, any job, when her mother needed such close monitoring?

She had briefly spoken to Sarah about her desire to teach riding as she needed a decent income to support her riding career. Her alternative career choices would have been primary school teaching or social work, but both involved many years at university, and she would still need an income to sustain either of those commitments, and she still needed time to watch her mother.

She could hear her mother now riffling through the cupboards — they were empty of what she was looking for. Laying aside her studies, she rose and picked up her shoulder bag.

"Come on, Mum. It's time to go out," Aimee said, trying to inject enthusiasm into her voice. "Let's go to that new shopping centre that's just opened and see what marvellous stuff they have." It was always the same ploy to get her mother out of the house, to distract her thoughts when she became restless. Take her out and make her tired before they came home, then they could both sleep well that night.

"No, I don't want to go out today. We went out yesterday, and you'll probably want to go out again tomorrow."

"I noticed they are starting up a craft centre near the shopping centre. I thought we might check it out."

"Why? You don't have time to join a craft centre with all you have on your plate."

Aimee' hands propped on her hips. *It's going to be a difficult day, again*, she predicted. "No, I thought *you* might like to join. There'll be lots of lovely ladies to chat to and you can get back into your painting – something you've wanted to do for a long time."

"No, I don't want to get back into that. It's a waste of time – and stop trying to get me into things to get me out of the house. Did you think I hadn't noticed?"

"You need to get out of the house, Mum. You can't just sit here day after day. You've done nothing since you lost your job. You need to stay busy." *You need to stay busy to take your mind off drinking, and I need you out of the house so I can concentrate on getting through my exams*, but she didn't say that. That would just start another argument. *Just keep her moving gently in a different direction*, she thought. *Something will come up.*

"How about we go to the hairdresser and get our hair done? Wouldn't you like that?" *Maybe you'll feel like getting another job if you start to look after yourself again*, but she didn't say that either. Things had been good for a while, but they were rapidly going downhill.

"How about we go shopping downtown?"

Straight away, Aimee tried to find an excuse not to. Their usual supermarket had a liquor outlet and so she avoided it, which is why she also didn't get to Sarah's as often these days as her mother would detour on the way home. Tomorrow would be soon enough for her to restock the cabinet, and she had to ride Monnie at least once this week. If only she could get there by a different route.

Thinking quickly, Aimee scooped the car keys up off the table and spirited them into her bag, thankful they did not clink and give her away. They could now not go anywhere until they found the keys. Sighing deeply, she returned to her room to study, to hide the keys, and to cry, and let her mother continue to search the cupboards, first for her needs, and then for her elusive car keys.

The following day, Rachael plonked down in a dark rage underneath the tree at Trailblazers, watching as Aimee led Monnie into the stable, saddled her up and checked her girth. Without looking back at her, Aimee mounted and headed to the far end of the paddock to ride listless laps as she stewed over the argument they'd had on the way there. Her mother had found the car keys in her room and the ultimatums had started to fly. She had to go shopping and Aimee would not be riding if she didn't get her shopping first! That meant, if she was to ride during the week, her mother would be drinking again.

Not wanting to discuss this with anyone, she had opted out of the lesson and needed to just be by herself to cry, and to make sure Monnie received some sort of exercise. This was something she had to sort out by herself: how to handle keeping her mother's mind off alcohol.

Partway into her third lap of walking, she noticed Sarah strolling across the paddock towards her. She halted closer to her, and waited.

"Hey, chicken, riding laps again?"

Aimee tried to smile, but guessed the tears in her eyes and on her cheeks would have made it pointless. She wiped them away.

"My head isn't in the right space for a lesson."

Sarah glanced back at Rachael. "Have another argument with Mum?"

Aimee sniffed. "It's nothing I can't handle."

Sarah's eyebrow rose. "By your demeanour, I don't think you're handling it too well. You will need to start working on your next test level if you are going to make a good showing at the next comp. Did you want me to pencil you in for a session on the weekend?"

Aimee felt all the air expel out of her. "I don't think I am ready to go up a level yet, Sarah. I just can't seem to get it together … and I need to spend more time at home with …"

Sarah sucked in a deep breath and let it out again. "Is it studies, or something else …?"

"Studies," Aimee lied, hoping Sarah couldn't tell.

"Okay," Sarah nodded, "but just ride some tighter circles to keep her flexible, and do some lateral work. Your studies will be over soon enough." She glanced back at Rachael, then back at Aimee. "If it's something else, I am here to help."

Aimee's face tightened and it took her a moment to meet Sarah's gaze straight on. "No, everything else is fine," she lied again.

Sarah left it at that and wandered back across the paddock, back towards Rachael, where she stopped for a chat before walking away.

Three days later, when the school bell rang, Aimee made her own way home as she'd been doing for some time now, the disappearing car keys ensuring her mother stayed home while she was at school. The last thing they needed was her mother getting caught driving with alcohol in her system. She hoped by keeping the car keys that her mother would be well enough to be able to drive her to Sarah's.

As she approached her house, she noticed an unfamiliar car parked in the driveway. Quickly, she raced in through the front door, only to see a familiar face talking to her mother.

"Hello, Theresa," Aimee said, very relieved to see her there.

"Hello, Aimee. I thought I'd pop in and see how you are both doing these days. I haven't seen you in such a long time. By the look of things, you need some help," she continued, nodding at her statement.

"Mum hasn't been well again," Aimee replied, fighting back the tears rising in her eyes.

"Aimee, I'm going arrange for Mum to go back into rehabilitation. Your mum has agreed to it because she really isn't feeling very well, but it does mean that you will have to go and live with Sarah again. Do you think there might be a problem with that?"

"All I can do is ask her," Aimee said, part of her feeling pain that her mother had relapsed, the other part feeling her energy restoring and her old life returning.

"Oh, I don't think it's going to be a problem." Theresa squeezed her hand. "Okay, I will make the arrangements now and we will see if we can get your mum admitted tonight. You go and ring Sarah and ask if she can have you tonight?"

"Sure, and thank you." Before she headed for the phone, she wrapped her arms warmly around her mother's neck. "Mum, we will beat this again, you'll see."

Rachael looked up with dull eyes, quietly whispered: "Hope so, but I feel so ill."

The ambulance arrived soon after, and Aimee watched her mother being wheeled into it, heading for another round of detoxification. She felt like crying, partly because her mother looked so ill – her skin now looked grey and wrinkled – partly through relief that help had arrived to comfort her through this situation, and partly through anger that her mother had let her down again. When the ambulance left, Aimee packed her belongings and waited for her angel to arrive to help re-establish some normality into her life.

The half an hour it took for Sarah to arrive felt like hours to Aimee. Theresa had already gone ahead to the hospital to complete the paperwork for Rachael's admittance.

"I am so sorry to have to put you through this again," Aimee said when Sarah walked through the door. "I am so sorry …"

"What are you talking about? I am delighted to have you back. It's going to be like old times, and we can get back into achieving those goals of yours. But for now, let's help you get back to your bright, happy self again and please remember that I am here for you if you need me." She closed her arm around Aimee's shoulder and looked directly at her. "That includes discussing any problems you might have. Understand, friend?" Sarah's smile reassured Aimee that all was indeed okay.

They arrived home, and Aimee immediately wandered out to the stables to say hello to Monnie. She now knew things were going to get better and that she'd be able to start pursuing her dreams again, but she also knew with the final exams only six weeks away, she had other priorities.

Aimee now began riding Monnie more regularly again, concentrating on perfecting the new movements for the next competition, which was thankfully after her final exams. She could therefore study hard, then ride and train to clear her head after each study session was over.

November arrived, and with it the exams, which took precedence over her riding for a time. Soon they were done, and she had a clear run to pursue her goals again, at least in the short term. She also now had to think more deeply about her options for the following year and how she would support herself, which she had discussed with Sarah.

"Don't worry about that right now," Sarah had said. "You can help out around here till your exam results are in … maybe you could teach a lesson or two to the newbies … and, of course, you need to stay available to visit your mum. We can discuss your long term future after the summer holidays when your mum is well enough to be involved."

Aimee felt pleased that weight had been temporarily taken off her shoulders. She now rode Monnie nearly every day, and they both improved to a point she felt confident in achieving good scores at Medium level. The competition in two weeks would clarify that.

The Sunday morning of the competition arrived, and Aimee bustled around getting everything ready as usual, her stomach bubbling with nerves and excitement as everything she had longed for came to fruition. Monnie had warmed up extremely well and Aimee and Sarah felt that she was ready to perform their first Medium test. She followed the usual gear check procedure, rode towards the entrance of the arena as she had done so many times before, concentrating on the smoothness of Monnie's stride and her willingness to obey the aids.

Aimee had entered A and delighted the onlookers with a beautiful square halt at X. The remainder of the test was ridden with absolute precision and grace until the final beautifully executed halt and the salute at the end. Aimee's wide smile told the whole story; she had ridden the test admirably, the best she had ridden yet. Sarah beamed from ear to ear and sighed that, after such a turbulent six months, Aimee was back to her true form.

They returned to the float where Aimee began to unsaddle and prepare for the journey home. Sarah's mobile phone rang.

"Hello, Sarah speaking."

"Hello, Sarah. This is Theresa. Is Aimee with you?"

"Yes, I'll put her on."

"Put your phone on speaker. You both need to hear this."

"Hello," Aimee said hesitantly.

"Aimee, it's Theresa. I have some bad news … your mother has lapsed into a coma and the doctors have said you should come and see her as soon as possible."

"What? Why? Is she going to be alright?" Aimee felt a cold chill wash over her.

"We're not sure, honey. That's why you should come now, straight away."

"Okay, we'll be there as soon as we can," Sarah interjected then rang off. "Get Monnie's boots on, Aimee, and put her on the float. I'll be back in a minute."

Sarah hurried over to the clubhouse to complete an envelope so that Aimee's test and results could be mailed out to her while Aimee loaded Monnie into the float for the trip home.

After bedding Monnie down, they headed for the hospital, confused as to how Rachael had deteriorated so quickly since their visit three days ago. They were directed to the Intensive Care Unit, where Rachael lay, many tubes coming out of her body and a monitor indicating her heart rate.

Aimee stood with her for a few minutes before being directed to the doctor's room behind the nursing station. She sat blankly, Sarah's hands on her shoulders as he explained the current situation. Aimee tried to fight the tears rising in her eyes, tried to swallow the lump growing in her throat threatening to choke her.

Having passed human biology at school with flying colours, Aimee understood the failing parts of the body the doctor referred to, which helped her understand the situation. But it didn't make her feel any better. She returned and sat by her mother's side for a few hours and spoke of the good times they'd shared, and the plans they'd recently made for the future, unaware of the lowering peaks on the monitor behind her. All the while, her mother lay peacefully asleep, seemingly enjoying her own world of dreams.

Then suddenly the ward lit up. An assortment of warning sounds broke the quiet. Immediately Aimee jumped up and back, allowing the doctors rushing into the room space around the bed. Sarah's open arms gathered her in, fearful of what was happening.

In the next seconds, a nurse ushered them out, leaving the doctors and nurses to help her mother.

"What's happening?" Aimee squealed. "What's happening?"

Sarah gathered her closer, turned her away from the activity around the bed. Another nurse pointed to the Waiting Room down the hall and Sarah guided Aimee there, entered and closed the door. "What's happening?" Aimee cried again, but Sarah could only shake her head, words at this time not possible. She prayed the doctors could work their magic, but everything had happened so fast.

"We just have to wait, Aimee. We just have to wait and see."

Aimee's tears streamed down her cheeks.

"We just have to wait and pray."

"She has to get better … she promised she would be with me to share my dreams. She promised."

An hour passed, most of it in silence. Then a doctor came into the room and approached Aimee. "Your mother is okay, for now, but she needs a kidney transplant urgently. We have put her on a dialysis machine until a donor kidney can be found. She can survive on the machine, but has to be under strict supervision for a while to ensure she 'follows doctor's orders'. This means she will be hospitalised for some time yet."

Then he explained the logistics of her treatment and where she would receive it. Aimee thanked him heartily then returned to her mother's side. Eventually they were encouraged to go home and sleep. The hospital would keep them informed of Rachael's condition.

Aimee kissed her mother on the forehead and reminded her that she loved her, and was sure she saw her mother's slight smile.

By now, Aimee had forgotten about the morning's events and began to think about her responsibilities to her mother when she returned home, which she casually mentioned to Sarah, hoping for her support.

"It'll be okay," Sarah said wistfully. "We will work through this together, and I'll help you as much as I can. You never know, your mum might miraculously come good. It's early days yet." She smiled reassuringly, knowing Aimee would be in for some tough times ahead.

Chapter 18

Future Dreams

Aimee very quickly fell back into the regular morning routine at Trailblazers, a routine she was now comfortable with. It was even better that she didn't have to go to school afterwards as her exams were over and she could concentrate on other things — like her mother, and her future. It would be months before she knew her marks, but she was confident she had done well, which would open up doors to a range of careers. She just needed to decide what she wanted to be.

She'd discussed her options with Sarah on several occasions but teaching riding and being a high-level coach was her ultimate goal. Already she could hear her mother poo-pooing the idea.

She had already given a few lessons for Sarah when Sarah had been occupied with a sick horse or a fallen rider, and she had really enjoyed helping young riders develop their skills. Mind, the students weren't much younger than she was. She realised they just hadn't had the opportunities she'd had to develop their skills under Sarah's daily instruction. Deep down, though, she knew teaching riding would not generate a lot of income — sometimes it was hit and miss if the weather turned ugly; sometimes riders cancelled — and she, therefore, needed to watch every cent she spent if she wished to compete at a high level without relying on Sarah for financial support — entry fees for competitions were very expensive — she obviously needed a steady income. She had also started to develop a rapport with some of her students; some had even asked if she would teach them next time.

Sarah had smiled on hearing that and had ruffled Aimee's hair. "You're a natural," she'd said, "and that shows you enjoy it, and because you enjoy teaching, the class will enjoy your lessons."

Riding Monnie more frequently, Aimee focused on being perfect at the level she was riding at and achieving some success at the level above. She had now conquered Advanced Level and had mastered movements for the Prix Saint George. Sarah had even been tempting her occasionally with a lateral or two from the Intermediare I and II level, taunting her that Monnie would get bored if she didn't keep posing challenges for her.

Competition weekends came and went with new successes and high scores, most times, building her towards her next goal.

Months passed with Aimee striving to improve hers and Monnie's suppleness and accuracy with each test they performed, all the while allowing time for Monnie to develop the muscles and fitness she needed for the higher level movements to avoid making her sore.

"A horse that becomes sore is a horse that becomes sour," Sarah had told her. "We climb the ladder slowly for the benefit of the horse. Oh, I know you are a natural, Aimee – I have never seen anyone come up through the ranks as fast as you have – the world will be your oyster. But remember, Monnie is your partner in this. Too soon, and she will want to throw in the towel."

Aimee didn't know what she meant by oysters in her world or throwing towels, but she understood Monnie needed time to develop physically, and she needed to be patient.

"Dreams are worth the wait." That was Sarah's catch-cry at the moment.

But I want it now, Aimee thought. *I need it to happen before it's too late and I miss my chance forever.*

As if Sarah had read her thoughts, she shook Aimee's shoulders one day at the table, giving them a good squeeze as she passed behind her. "Your time will come. To rush it is to ruin it. To stay long term in the game, you want to linger in the levels a little. You are steadily heading towards Grand Prix, and there is a big learning curve to get into that, for you and for Monnie. We have to get Monnie working really well on the double bridle and increase her collection work to include piaffe and passage. She will need to build more muscle to do that well and that will take time, and you need to be very subtle with your hands with the double reins so you don't hurt her. Intermediare II needs to become a walk in the park for you before you even think of stepping up from there, sweetie … and remember, you have your whole life ahead of you to achieve it. You're barely seventeen."

Sarah flicked the kettle on. "… and while you are lingering in the lower levels, give yourself the chance to be 'liked' by the other competitors. It's not just a matter of getting good scores … you need to get your name known and bandied about. Fame is part of the dream and getting your name out there is part of the big picture.' It was a part that Aimee hadn't considered.

Sarah made the coffees and returned to the table, set the cups down and looked at her earnestly. "Part of the big picture and big-time plans is sponsorship. If you are going to make it to the top and stay there, you need sponsors to help pay for this expensive dream of yours, and to get sponsors, you need your name out there. So don't be a fly-by-nighter – dabble in the levels for a while to get noticed. Your time will come soon enough."

Aimee sort of understood what she meant, and this was one of the most important talks Sarah had given her, which gave her plenty to think about.

She shook her head slightly. Sarah hadn't yet considered how she would cope with the pressure of being at the top of the game, and the dedication and effort it would take to stay there. While she was constantly competing against riders with a lot more experience – and this was also part of the learning journey – in her world, fighting against her dream was her mother's illness, and with each hospital visit, her mother looked worse. There hadn't been any improvement, and the lack of organ donors contributed to her mother's failing health. For weeks, Aimee had researched kidney failure and organ donations and what was involved; she had even spoken to Theresa about donating her own kidney if that would help. But Theresa had shaken her head.

"That's already been talked about. You are too young, and with your mother's past history of falling out of rehabilitation, they won't put you at risk. The doctors have said they won't consider it – it's totally out of the question … not at this point in time."

That had set Aimee thinking: even with a new kidney, would her mother be responsible enough to look after herself and stop drinking? Had this scare been enough to reverse her thinking? All the love she had given her so far hadn't made a difference.

All this ran through Aimee's head as Sarah talked about her future. Either her mother would deteriorate, and she would need to be at the hospital more often, or her mother would get well, and she would need to be at home with her.

She heard Sarah knocking on the table in front of her and looked up.

"Did you hear anything I said?" she asked, her eyebrows raised quizzically.

Aimee looked up and smiled. "Yeah, and I do understand. Then she frowned. There was just so much to think about.

So Aimee focused on her dressage, and Sarah introduced her

to more of the top riders at the competitions. They were out at events most weekends, either watching or dabbling in the higher levels as Aimee gained more experience – 'lingering in the levels' as Sarah had put it. Having gained impressive wins and high scores in Advanced, Aimee now set her sights on perfecting Prix Saint George; she worked out the muddle of using double reins and only using her fingers and back to send rein aids to Monnie as she worked towards Intermediare; she mastered flying changes every two strides and half pirouettes, which was indeed a big jump from Prix Saint George.

In between this training, Sarah inserted teaching her to drive, which came easy to her because, as Sarah said 'she had the gift of feel' – she could feel what the engine was doing and when the road conditions changed; she knew what it felt like to make a smooth curve and to look where she was going. Two weeks after her seventeenth birthday, on the day she passed her driving test, her mother came out of the coma.

As if everything in her life was now falling into place, Aimee won her first Intermediare II test against more accomplished riders. For weeks, nothing could wipe the smile from her face.

Chapter 19

An Emotional Time

Three and a half months later, just as she was preparing for bed, Aimee received a phone call. A donor had been found; her mother was going into surgery to receive the new kidney. She would soon have a new lease on life, and Aimee hoped she would cherish that opportunity.

Squealing with delight and a little fear, she roused Sarah, and together they rushed to the hospital, hurrying along the corridor in time to see her mother being wheeled towards the lifts.

"Mum!" Tears filled Aimee's eyes as she had feared she wouldn't see her before they took her to the operating theatre. The orderly stopped and Aimee bent down and gave her mother a good luck kiss on the forehead. "I love you," she said. "I love you."

"I love you too," Rachael replied huskily. "I'll see you soon," It was the happiest smile she had seen on her mother's face for a very long time, and hoped this was a prelude to a new life. From her research though, she also knew it was now a waiting game — they not only had to wait and see if the operation was successful, but also to see that the body did not reject the new organ. Aimee had been briefed months ago by the doctors of the procedure and the aftercare required when her mother left hospital, and was thankful there would be support helpers available. Aimee had also been warned to prepare for the commitment that was needed and that she should cherish whatever time she had left with her mother.

She and Sarah settled in for the long wait.

After five hours, the doctors emerged from the operating theatre, looking tired but jubilant. One entered the Waiting Room.

"Aimee, the operation went well," he said as he approached. "All is looking good at the moment, and we are just waiting to see that the kidney continues functioning as it should. But so far, it's looking promising."

Aimee hugged Sarah, and a tear escaped her eye.

"That's great. Thank you so much," Aimee gushed, trying not to cry. "How soon can I see her?"

"She's heading into recovery right now and will need to be fully stabilised before we can let you in to see her."

Aimee nodded.

More hours passed before the Recovery Ward nurse appeared. "You can come in now, love," she called. "She is asking for you."

Aimee walked into a ward divided by curtains. Her mother lay peacefully on the nearest bed, attached to various tubes and a machine that monitored her heartbeat. Nurses stood in strategic positions to watch the patients recently out of surgery. Sarah remained at the door as Aimee went forward.

"Hello, Mum," Aimee said as she reached her mother's side. She clasped her mother's hand and held it, concerned at how cold it felt. Her mother managed a small smile, and Aimee started prattling, reassuring her that she was in good hands; that everything went well, all the while hoping she wasn't telling lies.

Too soon, the nurses hinted it was time to leave so her mother could settle and sleep. They would take her up to a ward later in the morning and she would be in hospital for at least another week to ensure everything remained as it should.

Aimee breathed out a deep sigh. The operation had been a

success. She could return home … to Sarah's … as she now felt exhausted from the whole ordeal. She kissed her mother goodnight. "I'll be back later," she promised, then she and Sarah headed home.

Aimee drove this time and Sarah shielded her tired eyes as the sun came up. They fed the horses, together cooked breakfast, which helped relieve the anxiety Aimee had felt throughout the night. She huffed out another sigh, glad to be home where she could cast her mind onto other activities, which brought normality back in her life. And then she slept.

Aimee's alarm woke her in the mid-afternoon, and she rose immediately as she needed to ride Monnie before heading to the hospital.

She warmed Monnie up, varying the school figures as usual so Monnie didn't respond purely by habit, then she started riding smaller circles and diagonal lines to make her supple through her neck and shoulders, and more engaged through the hindquarters. But she would ride a movement then stop and walk for a while, finding her thoughts were not as focused as they should be. She would then ride another movement followed by another period of walking, Aimee's head still not in the right space for prolonged concentration. Her mind kept reflecting back to her mother hooked up to all the machines.

Realising it was pointless asking Monnie to work well when she was so distracted, she rode down to the paddock she now called 'Ambling Ally' and let Monnie relax on a long rein. It helped her own mood and, after twenty minutes, she returned to the stables to help prepare feeds for the horses.

"You're up," Sarah greeted her cheerfully, then said more seriously, "Are you okay?"

"Yes. I thought I'd work Monnie now so I could spend the rest of the afternoon at the hospital."

"That's fine, Aimee. I'll run you in when you are ready, but you'll have something to eat first."

Aimee nodded then dismounted and led Monnie into her stall and unsaddled her. After brushing her down and putting on her stable rug, she tossed the usual sections of hay into her hayrack then helped Sarah feed the remainder of the horses.

Over a meal of bacon, eggs and tomatoes, Sarah seemed rather quiet. Then she nodded as if agreeing with her internal conversation and said somewhat cautiously, "Aimee, I have an idea I'd like to run by you."

Aimee swallowed her toast and focused on Sarah. "Go on," she prompted.

"Would you be interested in breaking in some young horses to sell on. I'll give you fifty per cent of the profit of each sale, and that would bring you an income … I know you're concerned about expenses and this might help you out."

Aimee hesitated. She'd never ridden an uneducated horse before, let alone a young one.

"Where would they come from?" she asked.

"There's a stud farm up north that is disposing of all their stock due to the drought. If homes aren't found for them, they're going to be destroyed, and they come from such excellent bloodlines … I can't let that happen … to any horses for that matter. But these youngsters, with their bloodlines, shouldn't be hard to on-sell. I can do all the groundwork, but I need someone to ride and educate them once they are backed."

"You'll have to show me what I need to do," Aimee agreed, realising she still had a lot of learning to do. The memory of falling off Monnie flashed through her mind. "When do the horses arrive?" she asked.

"If you're in, I'll organise a truck to bring them down. We can put them in the very far back paddock until they settle in and gain weight. Then we'll work on them individually for the initial handling work. Don't panic. I'll show you whatever you need to know. Just be aware, it will be very different from riding Monnie."

They talked for the next half hour, discussing the technical side of breaking in and how Sarah expected Aimee to work with them. It sounded exciting, and Aimee felt a nervous tingle run through her, but she knew she had the best teacher in the world.

Aimee showered and changed into comfortable clothes, ready for a long visit at the hospital. Then Sarah drove her there, stopping on the way to buy a bunch of colourful flowers for Rachael.

Aimee hugged Sarah goodbye and made her way up to the Renal ward where her mother lay sleeping soundly, the machines still quietly monitoring every beat of her heart. She searched the ward cupboards for a vase and placed the flowers decoratively in it then pulled up a chair and sat beside her mother; held her hand and waited. An hour later, Rachael acknowledged her presence with a smile.

"Hello, Mum," Aimee said softly.

"Hello, darling. How are you today?"

"I'm fine. I am more worried about you. You look quite good today," Aimee lied.

They made idle conversation for a while, Aimee telling her about previous competitions and how Sarah had introduced her to some of the top riders in the state, who all seemed to know Sarah quite well. Then she started to tell her about the horses in the drought situation, but her mother fell asleep again and she sat gazing around the ward, noticing the many other patients, who were apparently in a similar situation. Some also had their families by their sides. Suddenly she didn't feel so alone but felt sorry for the other sick people who'd gone through a similar trauma. Then a hand landed on her shoulder and she looked up at the ward nurse beside her.

"Aimee, are you okay? You look a bit lost, love. I'm about to go down to the cafeteria. Would you like to come with me?"

Aimee glanced at her mother. She was still sleeping. "Please. That would be nice," she agreed.

Downstairs, Aimee bought a soft drink while the nurse had a cup of tea.

"So, how is Mum, really?" Aimee started the conversation, knowing how ill her mother looked and the brave front she'd been putting on.

The nurse stirred her tea. "She is doing okay, Aimee. She might not look as though she is, but she is doing okay so far. It will just take time for her to look at her best." She half smiled to assure Aimee of her truth. "Your mum will be with us for at least another week and you will see a big change in her in that time."

Aimee sighed then asked the question that had been prodding her brain for weeks. "So what do I need to do when she comes home? How do I look after her?"

The nurse smiled again, and nodded that she knew Aimee's concerns.

"You will have a programme to follow, and nursing staff will visit occasionally, and she will have medication to take – you must see to it that she takes it exactly as the doctor prescribes. There will be some life changes to your family, but nothing you can't manage. Many families have gone through this."

Then came the big question that had repeatedly been taking Aimee's focus. "What if Mum starts drinking again?"

The nurse looked up from her cup, sighed deeply and shook her head. "Let's just hope that doesn't happen, hey. It's a big ask for a girl your age, but you just keep an eye on her and she will have a new lease on life. As I said, your lifestyles may change a bit, but you will both work it out in the end." She smiled and glanced at her watch. "Ooops, I'd better be getting back. What I do want you to also think about, Aimee, is making sure you look after yourself during this process. Sometimes the carer gets forgotten. You will need to have good support behind you for that to happen." She downed the last of her tea. "I'll see you back upstairs." Then she was gone.

Aimee stayed, sipping on her drink as she thought about the nurse's comment. *She would need good support behind her* – but she had no one – no father, no family – all she had was Sarah, who had been so very understanding. She hoped that, if she needed support, this did not put a strain on their friendship. At least for the time being, the hospital would be that support.

By the time she had returned to her mother's side, Rachael was awake again. She reached out for Aimee's hand and they chatted for the remainder of the visit, her mother focusing on home life and planting a garden. Sadly, if Aimee mentioned Monnie or Sarah's new venture, her mother changed the subject. Then visiting hours were over.

Aimee bent over and gave her a goodnight kiss. "I'd better head down to meet Sarah," she said to avoid lingering. Goodbyes were just so hard.

"Honey, I've been thinking … now you have your licence, you could use my car. Then you don't have to put Sarah out anymore and you could move home … you're old enough to look after yourself now. We will have to change the insurance on it as it does not cover you at the moment."

"Oh, Mum, thank you." Aimee couldn't believe it. "I'm a very good driver, really, and I'll look after it. I promise."

"Well, it's no use to me here at the moment and I won't be allowed to drive for some time when I get home. You'd better bring the insurance papers in next time you come so we can get it sorted."

Aimee kissed her mum again, waved to the desk nurse and

made her way to the hospital exit to meet Sarah as arranged. When she explained to Sarah about the car, they detoured to Aimee's home to collect the papers, Sarah suggesting she didn't take the car until the insurance was organised, just to be on the safe side.

Chapter 20

A Rude Surprise

Aimee hadn't been home in quite a while, and knew the mail the neighbours had been collecting must be banking up. Feeling suddenly guilty, she dropped in next door to collect it.

Then, collecting the spare key from its hiding place, she entered through the front door and flicked on the lights. Immediately, she noticed the house felt empty. Emptier than usual. The television, the video and the stereo were missing. She hurried from room to room, checking to see what else had been stolen, then checked all the entrances to see where the thieves had got in. She'd seen enough movies to know not to touch anything and felt safer that Sarah followed directly behind.

They reached her mum's bedroom and noticed that her drawers had been opened and rummaged through. Aimee was unsure of what they would have found there. She returned to the lounge room, checked for other missing items but couldn't recollect what had been where and if anything else had been stolen; she felt quite relieved that nothing else major had been taken. Sarah phoned the police so Aimee could file an insurance claim while Aimee searched further to see what else was missing.

Then her mouth dropped open as she had a sudden thought. Racing past Sarah, she headed to the garage, hoping to see the little blue machine parked in its usual spot. A big sigh of relief escaped her that it was there. That was one problem she didn't have to worry about.

On returning to the house, she found Sarah staring at a photo she'd found in one of the cupboards in the lounge room. Aimee joined her, stood beside her in total amazement as she'd not seen the magnificently framed photo of herself on Monnie, obviously taken at the state championships. Her mother had not only failed to hang the picture, but she'd also not said anything about it. Instead, she'd just placed it in the cupboard on the bottom shelf.

"Why would Mum purchase such an expensive photo, frame it, and not say anything to me?" Aimee frowned.

"Maybe it was going to be a surprise for you for Christmas, or your birthday," Sarah replied, shrugging.

"The next question is … do I say anything to Mum about that, let alone the break-in?"

Sarah shrugged again. "Good question. But I wouldn't."

They remained at the house until the police arrived and a statement had been taken for the records. The police confirmed that the thieves were long gone and that they probably couldn't do much for them. Aimee then had to decide whether to leave the house vacant and return to Sarah's or commute back and forwards each day. She also didn't like the concept of being in the house on her own.

"You're not staying here on your own," Sarah made the decision for her, "not when someone obviously has access to the house. We will leave the lights on and in the morning we'll find a housesitter." Aimee agreed, thankful someone had made the decision for her. "Tomorrow, we'll come back and clean up and make it tidy. Right now I think we should call it a day. It's been a long one."

Aimee nodded, realising she now felt more than exhausted.

"Are you okay to drive?" Sarah asked her. "After this, I don't think you should leave your mum's car here. You can follow me home, and we'll park it up until the insurance is updated."

Aimee nodded again and yawned. At least the car would be safe if whoever had robbed them came back and realised it was there.

Chapter 21

The Dilemma

For the next week, Aimee rose early and worked Monnie before going in to visit her mother. She stayed as long as she could as her mother's condition hadn't improved much, but the nurses assured her there was nothing to worry about.

After a long moment of silence when they'd run out of idle chatter, Aimee's mother asked, "So how is your riding going?"

Aimee smiled. "Great. Monnie did a super full pirouette this morning."

Her mother smiled. "What's that?"

"That's where she turns a circle with her hindquarters in the centre of the circle and her forehand on the outside. She is getting better and better at them. Sarah says when she is really good at them, we can start working on passage."

Her mother smiled again, but Aimee realised it had gone way over her head. "What about you?" she asked, hoping she would be told the truth.

"I'm fine. Getting better all the time … feel better all the time when those handsome young doctors come around each morning."

"Mum!"

Her mother smiled a little wider. "You should come in early and meet a few of them."

"Mum!"

"Why not come in early on Saturday? There's more of them

on Saturday for some reason." Laughter lines creased her ashen face.

Aimee didn't smile with her – it was time to broach the issue with the weekend. She drew a deep breath. "I can't come this weekend, Mum. I'm really sorry, but there's a very important competition I need to ride in – it's for selection for the Nationals." She held back that the Nationals would be held in November in another state, and that she was desperate to be a part of the team.

"How lovely, dear." Her mother smiled genuinely, which surprised her – her mother usually changed the subject when it turned to horses – but this time she asked questions, which Aimee answered as best she could, knowing that her mother may not understand the lingo. "You will do well, I know it. You have worked so hard for it."

Her mother seemed so enthusiastic that Aimee wondered if she should mention the photo in the cupboard, but decided not to, in case she spoilt a surprise.

"I'm sorry I'm not going to be there for you," her mother added, tears welling in her eyes.

"That's okay, Mum. It's okay, and I promise I'll be in early on Monday to tell you all about it."

Her mother wiped her eyes. "You must thank Sarah for me for being there helping you through all this, getting you to where you want to be. I will make it up to her when I get home."

Aimee gave her a warm and prolonged hug. She noticed how frail her mother seemed at that moment, and wondered if she was indeed worse than she thought. She certainly tired quickly, even just talking made her breathless, which was not what she expected if her mother would soon be coming home.

When her mother started to drift off to sleep, Aimee kissed her goodbye, gave her another hug and left her to rest in peace. She stopped at the nurse's office on her way out.

"Hi, Jan," she said, having become quite friendly with all the nurses on the ward. "I'm worried about Mum. She seems so tired all the time. Is she really getting better? She still looks so ill."

The nurse flicked through Rachael's chart. "Yes, she's doing fine, Aimee. She's just tired at the moment due to the pain medication." Jan smiled. Aimee nodded, but it didn't fade the worry lines on her brow.

"I'll leave her to sleep then. You will call me if anything changes, won't you?" The nurse smiled and nodded. "I won't be in again until after the weekend. I have a major competition on Sunday, and it's important I do well," Aimee suddenly blurted out. Immediately, she felt guilty, wondering if she had sounded uncaring.

Aimee arrived at Trailblazers and immediately noticed a large truck parked at the back paddock. *The youngsters have arrived*, she realised and hurried down to help Sarah unload them.

She found Sarah supervising the stock handlers, handing them headstalls with a short rope attached so each horse had one on before clattering down the ramp to the field.

"If we don't have these on now, we won't be able to catch them again. They haven't had much handling yet," Sarah said as the last fine-legged youngster scrambled down the steep ramp, kicked up its heels and sprinted off to join the others, leaving a puff of red dust from its rump as it went. "They're pretty skinny," she added, "but they are certainly good quality."

Aimee felt excitement bubbling up inside her. "Oh, Sarah, they are beautiful." Even in their starved state, Aimee too could see the potential in each of them. They would be beautiful again under Sarah's care. "I'll go and get some hay for them."

Aimee raced off to the hay shed and loaded three bales onto the specially-made hay trolley and dragged it down to the paddock. Then Sarah beckoned her to the horse trough.

"We're going to soak the sections first," she said. "They will be so hungry I don't want them to bolt this down and choke on it. At least with it being wet, it won't stick in their throat so easily, and we'll scatter it out thinly so they can't grab huge mouthfuls. Everything is going to be 'careful, careful' with them at this stage." She stopped and gazed across the paddock where the youngsters were now milling together and sniffing out the best grass. "They certainly are beauties."

Her smile widened. "We did good, kiddo," she said, nudging Aimee in the ribs.

When the horses had found the hay and had settled into devouring it, Sarah and Aimee stayed at the paddock railing, watching for any issues, and scanning each horse carefully for injuries that might have occurred on the journey from the north.

"How was your mum?" Sarah finally asked in passing.

"Okay. She was tired, but the nurses said that she's getting better. Sarah, today she asked me a lot of questions about my riding. Do you think she now wants to become more involved, or do you think she is concerned about her mortality?"

"I hope that she's enthusiastic about your riding," Sarah replied, giving Aimee a concerned look at what she was thinking.

They watched the horses for another half-hour before agreeing they were okay and that the rest of their charges needed feeding; themselves as well.

As they headed for the house, Sarah said, "I've asked a breaker to come in to do the initial backing of the youngsters, Aimee, so that we don't get hurt, just in case they have a bit of a buck in them. I hope you don't mind. We will get them up to the breaking stage then Glen will take over for a week or so. We'll then continue on with their schooling. I thought this would be a safer option, as neither of us can afford to get hurt with the competitions that are coming up. Are you okay with that?"

"That's fine," Aimee agreed, slightly relieved that she wouldn't be getting on any bucking broncs. But something else had spiked her attention. "Where does Glen come from, and where do you know him from?"

"We met at some seminars about a year or so ago and I've heard some glowing reports about him. Apparently, he's so good with the horses and not harsh with them at all. He lives about ten kilometres from here, so he will come and go each day. This is his living, so he definitely knows what he's doing, which makes me feel a lot happier."

A big smile spread on Aimee's face. "That's great. Maybe he can teach us a thing or two."

With their risk now slightly reduced, they relaxed for the night, knowing their days would be busy over the next few weeks breaking in the new horses. Aimee also had a major competition to think about.

Chapter 22

More Butterflies

Sunday morning arrived with the usual butterflies fluttering in Aimee's stomach, as she could not afford to make any mistakes if she wanted to succeed in this competition. She couldn't understand how she could still get butterflies after all this time, but they were always there, right on cue.

An hour after loading Monnie on the float, they reached the Equestrian Centre, arriving three hours early so Aimee could watch the events before hers, and other competitors she would be up against. Many stunning horses were already being warmed up in the outdoor arena as she led Monnie into the stables. Returning to the car to collect the remainder of her gear, she heard a familiar voice calling, "Aimee! Aimee!!" and turned to see Susan hurrying towards her. She'd not seen Susan since school broke up.

They hugged then Susan helped her carry her gear back to the stables, prattling on as she went. "I opted for university after all," she said, "even though it means my riding needs to scale down even further: study has to come first. So I'm really surprised that Mum suggested I commit to this show and National selection. It'll really blow my studies if I get in. What about you? I know this means everything to you. Oh look, there's Monnie ... you beautiful girl."

Aimee smiled – things hadn't changed.

"I see you're riding Grand Prix today. Wow, you've come up

the ranks so fast – you must be the youngest rider ever to reach Grand Prix."

Aimee hadn't thought about that. She just went up the levels when Sarah said she should. Monnie was after all Sarah's horse, and Sarah was *her* coach – apart from the times she took her to the national coaches of the State Dressage squad for a special advancement lesson or a second opinion on her progress through the levels.

After securing Monnie in the stable and stowing all the gear in the locker, Aimee and Susan ambled off to watch some of the other competitors perform their tests. Together they had fun scoring the movements of each competitor and commenting on the execution of a movement and why it scored well or didn't – it helped them envisage how they would ride their test when the time came. Half an hour later, they agreed they needed to return to the stable and prepare their mounts for their respective events.

After brushing the gleam back on Monnie's coat, Aimee saddled up, stripped off her overalls, donned her tailored jacket and helmet and mounted. Then she rode to the warm-up area, wondering where Sarah had disappeared to. She hadn't seen her for ages.

The quality of horses that surrounded her in the warm-up area amazed her, and her mind immediately recalled the last time she'd ridden here, in this area, and rode with extra caution, staying clear of approaching horses. Monnie, however, was more settled and experienced now and continued to disregard all around her; she listened only to Aimee's aids as she worked her through various suppling exercises.

As Aimee trotted around the perimeter of the work area, she noticed a lady sitting in a wheelchair near the arena's entrance. At a brief glance, she thought it was her mother, but dismissed the thought as only a wish. On the next lap, she reined to a walk;

peered harder across the distance. The resemblance was so familiar that she stopped and pretended to pat Monnie while she assured herself of what she was seeing.

Then a squeal of delight erupted inside her and tears rose to her eyelids. "Mum!! Mum!!" Instantly, she tossed the reins over Monnie's head and vaulted off, and with Monnie trotting beside her, ran to her mother's open arms. Tears now spilled over.

"Mum, what are you doing here? This is a fantastic surprise!" Then she took in more of the surroundings. "Hello, Jan," she greeted the ward nurse who accompanied her mother.

"Hello, Aimee. Your mum needed an outing." She smiled.

"Thank you so much … and I am so pleased you are here, Mum, but are you well enough?"

"I wouldn't miss this for the world – I wanted to see my little girl ride and beat the best of them." She smiled and leant back and viewed Aimee more thoroughly. "My, you look gorgeous all dressed up like that, and Monnie looks fabulous too. You've certainly put a lot of work into your presentation. It's hard to believe my little girl is all grown up now." Then she glanced around. "How soon before it's your turn?"

"There's three ahead of me then I'm on. You are staying to watch, I hope".

"Absolutely. Jan and I will go and find a lovely place in the shade. Over there maybe."

Her heart beating furiously, Aimee remounted, waved to her mother, then, spying Sarah talking to someone over the far side of the warm-up arena, rode over to tell her the good news. Sarah quickly made her way to Rachael to watch Aimee's test with her and answer any questions she might have about the judging.

Soon enough, Aimee's name was called. She took a deep breath, patted Monnie's neck and uttered the words, "This one is for you, Mum."

Aimee steadied her breathing, settling the butterflies as she collected Monnie up beneath her. The sun shone gold across the wide-open field where the arena for her level of test had been set up, adorned with colourful flower boxes and white border rails, the sand base freshly graded after each competitor. The satin edging on her new black jacket glimmered slightly as the sun caught it, and her black boots gleamed. Even Monnie's neck and rump glistened.

Feeling confident at this level, Aimee quelled the butterflies, sent Monnie into a beautiful, supple, collected trot as she rode towards the markers at A. At X she saluted, and commenced her test. She could feel Monnie just bursting with energy, her quarters pushing her effortlessly through every movement, her neck and shoulders light and shifting to her slightest rein pressure. Knowing her mother was watching, Aimee rode as light as air, sitting tall and proud in the saddle. Her mother was watching her strive for her dream. What could be better than that?

When Monnie half-passed across the arena with absolute elegance and pizzaz, through the silence of the crowd she heard a gasp of delight from the shade of a tree, and on the next pirouette, loud clapping. Had it been so long since her mother had watched her ride? Had it been that long?

Riding like a breath of air, Aimee turned Monnie across the diagonal for the series of flying changes every stride. Effortless. Energetic. Monnie was enjoying herself too — she was showing off — which made Aimee smile. She once again felt like she was above the arena watching herself perform, seeing that visual of her being a champion rider. 'Ride the dream,' Sarah would say, and now she truly felt like she was riding that dream. Monnie was the dream, a magical, black, elastic horse taking her to the heights of perfection, and she glowed at the thought, reined this fluid magical creature in slightly for the turn, then let her out for a fully powered extended trot across the next diagonal. Power.

Floating. Exactly as it should be. She felt elated. As she rode past the shaded tree, she saw her mother standing, her hands on her cheeks, her mouth open and her face glistening with moisture.

Just in time, Aimee squeezed the rein and collected Monnie back into her hands for the turn. *Stay focused*, she reminded herself, *we're nearly there*. The test movements flowed back into her mind, and so did the visuals. One more half-pass across the short diagonal and they would be up the centre line to finish. *Stay focused. Stay focused.* She made the turn, powered forward, halted, felt Monnie ground her feet perfectly square, and drew a deep breath. She eased it out then saluted. The crowd that had remained silent for most of her test now stood and clapped vigorously, kept clapping as she left the arena on a long rein, Monnie's ears twitching at the sound, yet these days unperturbed by it. Aimee grinned widely, and a tear moistened her cheek that her mother had seen her at her best. This was a glorious day.

When she exited the arena, she noticed her mother's warm smile, as well as the tears in her mother's eyes, and hoped they were tears of joy.

"I'll just put Monnie in the stable and I'll be back," she told her mother as she rode past, not wanting to get too close to the wheelchair, just in case. Then she noticed Sarah wave her on to do so.

"Just drop her bridle off," Sarah called out. "You will need to be mounted for the presentations. She, therefore, had to keep Monnie ready to ride if she made it into the final placings. Patting Monnie exuberantly, she relived her test; felt the flow of the movements, and tried to pick any area where she might have lost points. It had all felt good to her, so there was a glimmer of hope of gaining a place, and to do so in front of her mother would be the candle in the icing on the cake.

Time ticked away, then the loudspeaker suddenly bellowed

into life, announcing the results of the Grand Prix test over the PA system. Aimee buried her face into Monnie's nose, praying as the place-getters were called out.

"In first place: Aimee Gardiner on Monique. In second place: Sarah Benson on Touch Down …"

No one heard the other results through the eruption of cheers and congratulations being shouted along the stable corridor. Aimee grabbed a tissue from her pocket and wiped away her tears as grooms and riders came and hugged her or kissed her cheek on her success. Others shouted from further down, "Good on you, Aimee," and "You deserve it, kid."

She almost sobbed. This was the dream of a lifetime, as she would undoubtedly be selected for the national team.

Rachael reached out to take Sarah's hand, shedding even more tears as she looked up at Sarah. "Thank you for all you have done. I am so proud of both of you."

Ducking back into the stall, Aimee put Monnie's bridle back on and led her out of the stable. Another competitor's groom bunked her back into the saddle and she headed for the presentation area. The remainder of her cheer squad – Sarah, Jan and her mum – were already settled at a strategic spot to view the presentations, Sarah and the nurse standing either side of her mother. The riders were directed to line up in front of the judge's box, in order of their placing. Aimee leant forward and congratulated each of the other competitors, who responded in similar fashion.

Then … "Ladies and Gentlemen … may I present the winners of the CDI-U25 Dressage competition," came the loud voice over the PA, "… but first a word from our wonderful sponsors of this event."

Dignitaries were introduced, each giving a small speech about how happy they were to support the event and the quality of riders that had performed today, and the interstate judges acknowledged how impressed they were with the competition standard. Then came the important part: each placegetter from lowest to second place were presented with their coloured sash.

Then Aimee's name was called and she nudged Monnie forward. A wide coloured sash was placed over her head and shoulder, and a huge trophy and an envelope were handed to her. She reined Monnie back into the lineup, waited for the signal to move off for the Lap of Honour, praying she wouldn't drop or break the trophy.

"Ladies and Gentleman, before the riders move off for the Lap of Honour, we have another special announcement to make, and that is the team selection for the National championship to be held in Perth in November."

With that, four other placegetters from the other events rode into the arena and stood behind the lineup. A hush fell over the crowd again.

"They are as follows:" the announcer continued, "The senior team will be Helen Mount on High Tower, Aimee Gardiner on Monique, and Tracy Bell on Lieutenant Commander. The reserve is Simon Hock on Legendary.

"The junior team will be Isabelle Troop on Best Friend, Sarah Smith on Little Ebony and Faye Smithen on Superman. The reserve is Robert Smyth on Deep Pocket.

"Congratulations to you all, and on behalf of everybody here, we would like to wish you all the best of successes over there."

Aimee looked around and saw her mother tightly squeezing Sarah's hand; she was still holding it when she came out of the arena, which revealed another of her dreams had come true — her mother and Sarah were becoming good friends.

Numb with joy, she now had more than she had ever wished for.

Back at the stables, Sarah took Monnie and began to

unsaddle her while Aimee attended to an endless crowd of people gathering to congratulate her. Rachael stood by with the utmost admiration.

Amongst the crowd was an official who patiently waited to invite Aimee and her family back to the meeting room for the obligatory celebration drinks. Rachael declined as she was beginning to tire, and Jan felt they should return to the hospital as it was time for Rachael's medication.

"Aimee, I am so proud of you," Rachael said as she hugged Aimee warmly. "This has been the best day of my life and I thank you for making it so special for me. I love you." Aimee prolonged the hug, thanked Jan for her support then walked with them to the waiting car.

When she returned to the stable, Sarah said, "Aimee, this is your day … you go up to the celebration. I'll pack the car up and join you shortly."

"No, we'll do it together. I wouldn't be here if it wasn't for you," Aimee replied, and together they packed the mountain of gear back into the car, filled up Monnie's hay net so she was occupied in their absence then made their way up to the meeting room where Aimee blushed at the raucous round of applause she received when she entered.

Aimee and Sarah moved from cluster to cluster of competitors and their families, all excited about their achievements on the day. Individual tests were dissected, errors admitted, yet the general comment on Aimee's test was it was perfection, which further swelled her confidence. The only thing missing was her mother being there with her to celebrate.

Eventually, as dusk shadowed the windows, and the congratulatory speech from the president of the Equestrian Federation was over, Sarah and Aimee drifted back to the stables to take Monnie home to rest in the security of her own comfortable stall.

The hour-long trip home felt like two hours, their wide smiles not reducing with the distance, yet they sighed in unison when the large front gate welcomed them home. With Monnie tended, and all other chores completed, they sat down to a well-earned canned meal on toast, both agreeing they didn't need to be nutritionally conscience until tomorrow.

"I heard your name being bandied around today," Sarah told her softly over the customary cup of Milo after the meal.

"What? Who by?"

"Mmmm … I think there might have been some sponsors in the crowd. A few approached me and asked more about you. It's all paying off, Aimee." She smiled into her cup, then looked up at Aimee, whose eyes were now twinkling. "You're a step closer to your big dream."

Hearing Sarah say it made it all the more real, and Aimee's head spun with possibilities, with visions of riding in the Nationals. Of knowing her mother was watching her and cheering from the sidelines. She was so close to having it all.

Thinking of her mother, she picked up her cup and headed for the phone. "I'm just going to ring the hospital and see if Mum is still awake … and make sure she made it back to the hospital okay."

Sarah looked up and nodded.

Rachael had now been transferred to a normal ward, where the desk nurse could transfer her call to her room after checking that the patient was awake. Aimee was delighted to speak to her mum directly.

"Hi Mum, how did you recover after today?"

"Hello, my wonderful champion. I'm fine; a little tired, but fine. What about you? Have you recovered from your fantastic win? I've been telling everybody here all about it and they are just as proud as I am. I want to do that again when I get a bit better," Rachael replied honestly.

"Mum, slow down. Today was the greatest thing you have ever done for me, and I just wanted to say 'thank you' for doing it. My win was because of your support, just knowing you were there. You know that, don't you?" Aimee said

"You are the one with the talent, darling. Not me. And you were the one riding Monnie, not me so, therefore, you deserve all the credit, and of course, Sarah deserves a huge amount of credit for getting you to where you are. Please pass on my congratulations to her for doing such a wonderful job."

"I will. Thanks again, Mum. I will let you go now as you are probably very tired. I know I am."

"Goodnight, my champion. I look forward to seeing you soon."

Aimee hung up the phone, relieved that her mother was well and that she could now go to bed and have a good night sleep, even with the replay of the day's events and images of her new win swimming around in her head.

"Thank you, Sarah," she hollered from her bed as she turned out the light.

Further down the corridor, Sarah smiled.

Chapter 23

The New Experience

Over the next few days while Monnie rested after her stunning performance, Aimee and Sarah started work on the youngsters. Standing in the paddock, with lead ropes over their shoulders and pocketfuls of grain in their jackets to tempt them with, they stood screening which ones would be the first to handle.

"What about that dark chestnut with the blaze?" Aimee suggested. "He looks like he's already put on some weight."

Sarah cast an experienced eye over him and nodded. "Good choice, but I think I'll start with the brown with the star. He has a kind eye so hopefully won't be too much trouble."

Separating, they moved across the field in different directions, keeping a close watch on the small group that had now become familiar with them and that now milled around, looking for the food they were used to getting. During feeding times, they had both been able to occasionally run a hand across their neck or face, a gentle touch that did not pressure or threaten them. When Aimee's chosen horse came closer, she stood still and waited, knowing the smell of the grain would draw him into her. She had been preparing the horses for catching for days, always having a nice handful of grain or cubes in her pocket to offer them.

Once the horse was feeding from her hand, she clipped the end of the lead rope to its headstall and the chestnut was suitably caught without a fuss. She now had to remove herself and the horse from the group without being kicked or bullied by the other horses hoping to get some grain. Across the field, Sarah had also taken hold of the brown filly and was backing away from the others.

"Just lead him around the paddock for a while, Aimee, and turn in different directions so he gets used to watching you and staying with you. Thankfully they are used to being handled to some degree at the Stud." She did the same, moving the horse around her, touching its side to move it away, and ensuring the brown horse focused on her. Soon the other four youngsters wandered off to graze, and Sarah indicated it was safe to leave the paddock and head up to the round yard.

"Our job today is to see how much they've been handled and teach them to tie up," she said as they led the two into the round yard. "I'll start this little lady off first at the tie off post, if you want to get those brushes and start gentling him by brushing him down. Do it while you are holding him so he feels he can move away if he feels unsafe, and don't do his legs and underbelly yet, just neck, sides and topline – we will work on the legs only after they are totally happy with the brushing and trusting us."

Aimee led the youngster outside the round yard to watch Sarah as she began the brushing lesson. It was not wise to have the two horses in the round yard together as, at this age, they could be unpredictable.

Then Sarah moved the filly over to the tie-up post, placed a wide, thickly padded strap with large loops on the ends over the dusty brown neck and secured a rope to the loops. Then she tied the other end to the very thick post with a quick-release knot, just in case, all the while talking soothingly to her.

"We really need to give them names," Sarah realised as she slid her hands gently down the filly's neck and backed away so the filly could test the rope and do whatever she decided to do.

Sometimes they just accepted being secured; other times they erupted and fought the rope until they realised the only way to reduce the pressure on their neck and head was to stop fighting. Sometimes they threw themselves on the ground, and this Sarah warned Aimee to be ready for and that her quietly standing chestnut might leap and react if that happened. "Regardless," Sarah added, "always keep your hand on the horse so you can feel if it is coming your way and you can move with it rather than be knocked over."

Aimee watched Sarah with admiration as she worked with caution and confidence around the tense filly. Her hands though soon brought it to leaning into her hands and brush. The session was short and without eruption, Sarah explaining that to put them back in the paddock wanting more pleasurable sensations, like the patting and the brush, would encourage them to come in more freely next time. So for the next few hours they caught and handled each of the rescued horses, using the same routine. This became the daily task for the week, and soon, the horses stood at the gate waiting patiently for their turn.

Aimee had given them each a name, relating to their temperament or looks. Occasionally she snuck in a movie character which she thought was apt. They started with the chestnut which they called Munchkin as she always looked like she could be unpredictable, and the brown horse became Thor as he was quite stocky and good looking.

The following week a soft bit was placed in their mouth and they spent time in a stall, becoming accustomed to confinement and to having the bit in their mouth. The brushing continued, then they were turned into a smaller paddock away from the others, and allowed to graze for an hour wearing the bit, all in preparation for riding.

This daily routine kept Aimee and Sarah busy and too exhausted to think about much else, including regular visits to the hospital to visit Rachael. Aimee felt she would not be good company when it came to holding a conversation with her mother. Instead, she would phone her mother at the end of the day to give her a daily progress report. Rachael seemed delighted with the news but always mentioned that she missed Aimee visiting.

The next day began early with Aimee working Monnie at seven o'clock. The air was crisp and there was not a cloud in the sky, and Aimee's concentration drifted into the land of serenity where she had always felt the happiest. Monnie seemed to understand as she too worked exceptionally well. Completing their training session, they both seemed thoroughly contended. *A good way to start the day*, Aimee thought.

She led Monnie down to her usual paddock then made her way back up to the house for breakfast. She could smell the bacon and eggs from the doorway. That just topped off a great start to the morning.

Having let the new horses recover from the mouthing, she and Sarah were outside, ready to continue long reining 'the babies', as they were now called. They began with Thor, the dark brown gelding, who appeared to have the best temperament. Aimee held on to Thor's bridle while Sarah took up the two reins and started walking him around the arena while Sarah applied rein pressure to indicate the direction she wanted Thor to go. Much to her surprise he accepted being directed without any resistance and mastered the task well. As usual, they kept the session short to avoid boring him.

Aimee returned him to the paddock while he still responded well to the stopping and starting on command. Aimee had also begun teaching them to respond to her body movements – so if she stopped, so did they.

Aimee then caught Munchkin. At the end of that session,

Aimee and Sarah agreed they deserved a coffee break before handling Ethan, who was clearly a double agent as he wanted to do things his way. The day progressed in this manner, and they managed to do all six horses by late afternoon, feeling very pleased with what they had accomplished.

Although it was late afternoon, Aimee agreed she should go and see her mother before the day was over. She showered, changed and made her way to the hospital.

Rachael lay on her side in her usual bed, just laying staring out the window.

"Hi, Mum. Are you okay?" Aimee asked, suddenly concerned.

"I don't feel too well, love. The doctors seem to think I overdid my physiotherapy session as I thought I was tougher than I am, but it was all worth it as I want to be home with you. I should be right in a couple of days," she continued weakly.

"As long as everything is okay," Aimee said, frowning.

They talked for the next hour, Rachael listening to Aimee's excited descriptions of breaking in the youngsters and all she was learning from Sarah. Filtered into this was her plans for the future, and Aimee smiled inwardly that her mother seemed more positive about her future and was keen to make plans with her.

By the end of the hour, in which Aimee had yawned widely several times, Aimee apologised for not staying longer, but realised she was exhausted and needed an early night. Her mum nodded and suggested that was a good idea.

Aimee returned home to find Sarah watching TV with a warm cup of Milo on her lap. "Your dinner's in the oven. Sorry I didn't wait, but I was starving."

"All good," Aimee replied, grabbing an oven mitt and retrieving her dinner from the oven. She sat down with Sarah and relayed the conversation she'd had with her mother, Sarah pleased that Rachael took more interest in her daughter.

"Glen is arriving tomorrow to take a look at the babies," she announced. "He should be here about ten o'clock so we'd best get an early night. Tomorrow will be busy."

"It has been a busy month preparing the babies for this moment," Aimee said, nodding.

"Yes," Sarah replied. "But it will be worth the effort."

Chapter 24

An Even Bigger Surprise

The morning began as usual, except this time there was no smell of bacon and eggs wafting through the doorway, only toast and jam accompanied by a warm cup of Milo as Sarah was keen to start on the babies.

"What's the rush?" Aimee asked.

"Glen will be here at ten o'clock and I want to make sure we have lunged most of them by the time he arrives," she explained.

"If you lunge that big cuddly teddy bear, Barney, in the arena I will work Louie, the regal one, in the yard at the back of the stables.

"Then Glen can handle them," Sarah continued. "Oh, and I meant to tell you … I may already have a buyer for Ethan," Sarah said as they headed off to fetch their respective horses.

"That's good news. Are they aware of just how uneducated he is?" Aimee asked.

"That's what they're after. Their daughter has to school a young horse for her 'A' pony club certificate, and they think Ethan might be perfect. They are coming out to see him next week."

As the babies had certainly got the hang of lungeing, in five minutes both horses had settled into some active, obedient work. Sarah then decided to cool them off ready for Glen.

As Aimee untacked Barney, she noticed out the corner of her eye a handsome man, armed with a stock saddle, a body protector and a helmet walking towards her. She immediately signalled to him that Sarah was in the stables. She also noticed Sarah's eyes light up when she saw him.

"Hello, stranger! Fancy seeing you in this neighbourhood," Sarah said as she hurried down the corridor to greet him.

"Yep, it's been about twelve months," Glen reciprocated, smiling. "I heard you still make a great cup of coffee."

Aimee stopped ungearing Barney and watched as her friend and the handsome man hugged lightly. She wished she was twenty years older.

"Glen, this is Aimee," Sarah said. "She's sort of my adopted daughter, and is also going to be the next Australian Dressage champion," she continued.

Aimee blushed as the man turned his attention to her, and also at what Sarah had said – she was sort of an adopted daughter. She never knew Sarah had felt like that. "Come on then, let's go in and coffee up before we start with the babies."

"Good idea." Glen grinned, a wide smile Aimee melted over.

Morning tea was short and sweet, with everyone keen to get to work, Aimee just keen to see Glen ride as she hoped he rode as well as he looked. Sarah just smiled all the time.

Sarah went to the stable and retrieved Louie who had cooled down considerably from his lungeing. Glen led him out to the round yard and moved him around him, both forward and backwards just using hand signals.

"You girls have done a great job," Glen said as he ran his hands over Louie and picked up each foot in turn. Then he slipped Louie's bridle on and led him around a few circles, again poking him around with a finger, backing him up and walking away from him to see if Louie would follow. Louie did. Then Glen walked to the rail and put on his helmet.

"Today is just a layover session so he gets used to my weight, and it's all hands-on, hands-off. As soon as he stiffens to what I am asking, I'll back off so he feels he can escape if he needs to. He will accept me quicker the next time because he's not being forced or restricted. Everything must be pleasant for him." Glen kept his hands moving across Louie's coat, then draped his arm over Louie's back, and leant against him. After doing this several times, he led Louie over to the railing, stepped up onto the lower railing and laid his bodyweight over the horse's back. Louie flinched but remained in place. Then Glen turned the horse's head towards him and patted his face, while he stayed laying over its back. The horse stayed there, but his ears flicked in all directions.

Sarah and Aimee remained well back from the railing to stay out of the way and not distract the horse while Glen worked gently with him. After a while, Glen slid his feet back to the ground then repeated the action, Louie flinching less, and Glen nodded his delight. "He's taking everything in his stride. We won't have any issues with him," he said as he dropped back to the ground and made a fuss of Louie. "The next step for him is to put a saddle on him and take him for long walks to prepare his back. If he accepts that alright, I should be able to mount him by the end of the week."

Barney was not so obliging. He leapt around and tried to run away, until Glen's calmness encouraged him to be more accepting.

"Who is this one"? Glen asked as he swapped Barney for the next horse.

"This is Annie," Sarah explained. "She's very humanised. I'm sure she'd sit on the lounge and join you for pizza if you allowed her to."

The next horse, Munchkin, showed she had thorns and demonstrated her ability to be nasty; she gave an immediate buck to show her unwillingness to oblige. Then she started a tug of war, but Glen kept going back with her until she could see no point in backing up anymore. She then submitted to this man who gave her no reason to fight or flee.

By now it was lunchtime, and all three adjourned to the kitchen where Sarah and Aimee prepared cold meat and salad with fresh rolls.

"I see you've become domesticated," Glen quipped to stir Sarah up. He winked at Aimee, who sat admiring the male scenery in the room.

Sarah countered him perfectly. "So, Glen, how is Monica these days?"

"Don't know … haven't seen her for seven months," he shot straight back.

Sarah turned and looked straight at him. "I thought you two were inseparable," she replied, happily astonished.

"So did I until she ran off with some lawyer. I hope he's doing to her what they do to their clients." He laughed.

"How do you feel about the situation now?" Sarah asked more caringly.

"I have realised that I'm better off without her. I actually have more money in the bank now and am really enjoying life." He continued to gaze at Sarah. Aimee's mind drifted to the morning's events.

"How about you? Are you seeing anyone?" Glen asked.

Aimee stopped eating her sandwich and looked at Sarah. This was not a situation she'd ever discussed with Sarah.

Sarah didn't notice.

"No. I haven't had the time to find anybody," she said matter-of-factly. Then they both launched into a conversation about the previous years and what they'd both been doing with their lives. Sarah's conversation involved Aimee as she explained to Glen how Aimee had become an important part of her life. Glen thought that was a great idea and congratulated Sarah on being a great 'Mum'. They all laughed.

The afternoon crept on and Glen resumed working with the remaining two babies, each having a temperament similar to Louie and were quite easy to work with.

With the last baby returned to the paddock, Aimee worked Monnie before going to the hospital to see her mother, Glen lingering to watch her ride, having seen all her accolades in the family room trophy cupboard, then he helped Sarah prepare the night feeds. She could hear Sarah laughing and chatting with Glen as they fed the tribe of horses and completed the chores required at a riding school.

Sarah and Glen sat on the house verandah enjoying a cold soft drink when Aimee returned to the house to shower before visiting her mother.

"Glen …" she heard Sarah hesitate before asking as she headed inside, "I don't suppose you'd like to stay for dinner."

"No, definitely not!" Glen shot back. Then he smiled. "But I'd like to take you out for dinner … if you have no objections."

Sarah smiled. "How could I refuse such an offer."

As Aimee came back onto the verandah, Sarah hurried towards her. "I'm in to shower and change," she said, her eyes bright to the point of twinkling. "Don't wait up for me."

Aimee grinned. "You two just behave yourselves," she retorted then hugged Sarah goodnight.

Glen waved Aimee goodbye and watched her drive away.

Aimee's visit to the hospital was brief as Rachael didn't feel or look well, and their conversation was quite disjointed even though Aimee did most of the talking. Eventually, she made up an excuse and left, which Rachael didn't mind as she was feeling very tired.

Chapter 25

Great Friends

The following days became routine, with Glen taking the next steps to mount the babies while they remained standing still. Each session, he stepped up via the stirrup and either swung off to the ground or lowered himself to the ground very gently via the stirrup so he didn't scare them. Aimee and Sarah prepared the horses for him to change to, sometimes lungeing them first to take the edge off before Glen commenced work.

Aimee lingered at times, watching closely, keen for the time she would start riding the young ones, and knowing there was a lot she had to learn – riding uneducated horses was so incredibly different from riding an educated horse, especially a Grand Prix level dressage horse.

Towards the end of the week, Aimee hung over the railing watching Glen riding Annie, the quietest baby, around the arena. After a few laps of stopping, starting, walking and trotting, he halted at the rail beside her and smiled.

"Your turn," he said, dismounting slowly and giving Annie a pat.

Aimee's heart leapt in her chest. It was time! She was going to ride the youngsters! Fetching her helmet and body protector, she climbed through the railing a little way away and secured her helmet as she reached Glen, her heart still galloping.

"Take your time mounting," he said as she slipped the reins over Annie's head.

Aimee placed her foot in the stirrup, being careful not to jab the filly's side with her toe, and landed gently in the saddle. Annie's ears twitched back at her – she knew someone different was on board. Aimee eased out a breath and tried to relax.

"Now, keep your legs against her. As long as you have your legs on her, you have control. You've got good hands, but just be sure not to jab her in the mouth if she leaps into the upwards transition. If she begins to slow down without you asking, tap her with the whip and apply your legs stronger so she learns this means 'forward'." He placed Aimee's legs firmly on Annie's side. "Okay, nudge her on."

Aimee did as Glen requested, and soon realised how unbalanced and gangly Annie felt and how little steering control she had compared to Monnie.

"Drive her forward," Glen yelled out as Annie trotted with reluctance down the long side of the arena, sometimes going slightly sideways.

"This feels really weird," Aimee laughed as she began to ask more of Annie.

"Well done, Aimee," Glen responded. "Now ask her to turn and do some very large circles."

Aimee guided Annie onto a circle that looked more like an egg than a circle. "I feel like I don't have proper steering control," Aimee called back.

"You haven't, but that will come when she finds her balance," Glen replied. "Try lowering your hands, thumbs turned out and use a low open rein to guide her around, and weight your inside stirrup more. But stay upright and urge her forward."

Aimee continued to ride for another fifteen minutes, working on turns, circles and walk to trot transitions, the filly responding amazingly well when ridden as Glen instructed. It seemed a whole different way of riding, accentuating the subtleties she used when riding Monnie. She now looked forward to applying Glen's methods to the other babies – she was learning so much.

Glen encouraged Aimee with precise instructions for each youngster she mounted, while Sarah sat back in the shade watching, having declined the offer to have a ride yet in order to not risk her back until they were calmer.

"No, thanks. I've done enough of these in my time," she'd quipped. "I'll let you two have all the fun."

They spent the day working with the babies and watching them progress through the stages of their education. By now, the babies were accustomed to the daily routine and seemed to look forward to their session, even enjoying the hose down they were given at the end of each lesson. They were always rewarded with a bucket of chaff and carrots, and this part they appreciated most as their ears flicked in the direction of the feed room as soon as they entered the stables.

Glen had become part of the team now and Aimee noticed he seemed to spend more time at Sarah's than at his own place, and Sarah's smile never seemed to leave her face. But the time was fast approaching when Aimee could take over the training of the babies, and Glen's expertise would not be required as much as before.

"Sarah, how much longer are we going to need Glen?" Aimee bravely asked when Glen was out of hearing range.

"Now that's a good question. Do you think we had better get some more babies in?" Sarah asked, her smile widening.

"Well, he does improve the scenery," Aimee quipped back, suspecting Sarah felt the same.

"I know he has another stud to go to next week, but I think we will have to always get his expert opinion about things. Won't we?" Sarah smiled.

Glen arrived back and joined them on the verandah where they usually sat recovering from the long day's work with refreshments and their feet up on the railing.

Glen flipped the lid off a cold can of Coke and sighed deeply. "We are pretty much at the end of the line with them now," he admitted, somewhat dully. "There's nothing much I can do now that you and Aimee can't do." He downed a mouthful of drink and stared out across the garden and stable complex further over.

Sarah sipped her cold Milo then eased the cup back onto the table beside her. "What do you have on next?" she asked him without much enthusiasm.

"I've got some work on a stud over in Whitmore — a string of yearlings needing their first handling, then some two-year-olds needing backing. You should see the place — it's all white fencing and American style barns. They must be worth a pretty penny."

Aimee reached over for a handful of chips and noticed Glen had reached out and grasped Sarah's hand. Her eyebrow raised and a smile hinted at her lips. *This is getting serious*, she thought.

"It's about a month's work, but I want to be around to see the babies go to their new homes, whenever that will be. You will call me when the time comes?" he said, looking at Sarah.

She nodded. "Yes … yes, of course." Then she subtly smiled.

Glen heaved out a breath and nodded. "I feel I have a vested interest in these babies now … if you know what I mean."

Aimee rocked back in her chair, her smile spreading wider as she glanced again at Glen and Sarah.

Chapter 26

Decision Time

Two months later, Sarah advertised the babies for sale. The horses looked stunning and, though still needing more education, they were amiable under saddle and worked well at the basic level. With Sarah's popularity in the local horse industry, word soon passed around that she had some well-bred youngsters for sale.

A flood of enquiries poured in, both personally and via the phone. Prospective buyers came at all hours of the day to view the horses, some wanting to ride, some just to observe how good they were, some just coming for a joy ride – just wanting to ride a horse without having to pay for it. But Sarah didn't mind – it was good experience for the babies to cope with different riders. Sadly, the first horse sold was, not surprisingly, Annie, who went to a lovely pony club home. The young girl was about to outgrow her existing pony and needed a new one for the next year. Annie was perfect in every way, and she soon headed off to her new home with some very happy owners. Aimee gave her a prolonged hug and a kiss, feeling sad at losing her, as she was loaded onto the float.

Then Munchkin went, the interested party making their mind up quickly and happily buying him. Another pang of sadness touched Aimee and Sarah, who had both become attached to all of them. But the babies had been purchased for on-selling and were an important source of income, so they had to be sold.

Every horse on the place had its price and would ensure Trailblazers would eventually be owned outright for Sarah's retirement.

So now only Barney, Thor and Louie were left, and the line of interested customers kept coming, some agreeing to leave them with Sarah for a bit more education. Consequently, Aimee consistently worked them till they became more balanced at walk, trot, and canter, smoother through the paces, and cantering on each leading leg on command – effectively ready to compete at preliminary level.

Sarah and Glen were pleased with their progress and commended Aimee on her brilliant work, Glen frequently visiting to see how things were going, and, as he said, 'to be on hand should they have any issues': Aimee just smiled – she wasn't blind.

Just after lunch one afternoon, Aimee headed out the door to school Louie before she worked Monnie. Louie had progressed the most out of all the youngsters and therefore had the least major contrast to her beautiful black champion. As she and Sarah walked out the back door, a gentleman, neatly dressed in a suit and tie, walked across from the driveway towards them. He was tall and looked to be in his early forties.

"Hello, are you Sarah?" he called out.

"Yes, may I help you?" Sarah replied.

"My name is Michael Trustcott and I am interested in buying one of your horses."

"Certainly. Come this way and I will show them to you," Sarah responded.

"No. Not 'them'. I have a particular mare in mind. A horse called Monique. My clients prepared to pay generously for her."

Sarah and Aimee stopped abruptly. Their mouths dropped open. This situation had never been contemplated. They glanced at each other, Aimee's mouth going dry.

A coldness washed over her, and her eyes started to burn. *Not Monnie!* she thought.

Michael broke the silence. "My clients are prepared to pay $50,000 for her."

Sarah heaved out a loud breath. Aimee stood gobsmacked.

"I don't know what to say. I would certainly like some time to think about this, as Aimee has been selected to represent the state at the Nationals in two months' time," Sarah said, her voice slightly tremulous.

"That's not a problem. They want Aimee to continue riding her for now, at least till after the Nationals. They just want to own her and breed from her in two years' time," Michael replied.

The man reached into his suit coat pocket, drew out a purchaser's contract and handed it to Sarah. "You see, the offer is genuine. You can see it states who the owners will be, but promising Aimee can continue to ride her in future competitions."

Aimee noticed Sarah's breathing had heightened. She felt the blood drain out of her face. Selling Monnie would pay off half of Sarah's mortgage – but Monnie … Monnie was like … hers. She had ridden Monnie for four years; it was like Monnie was her horse now, not Sarah's. *This can't be happening!* She was so close to achieving her dream with Monnie – her and Monnie, together they were a team –they would go to the top together.

But this was a deal Sarah couldn't afford to refuse. The money would certainly help their financial situation, but it would also mean she could lose Monnie in the next few months.

Seeing their dilemma, Michael left the contract with them, with a promise to return the next day for an answer.

Sarah and Aimee stood shaking their heads as they watched him walk back to his car, Aimee forcing back tears and thankful he did not ask to see Monnie that day. She couldn't have coped with that at all.

They stood for a long while after the car disappeared down the driveway, Sarah still staring in the direction it went, Aimee staring at Sarah, waiting. Finally, Sarah lowered her chin to her chest and heaved out a breath.

"I don't feel like working the babies right now," she said. "Let's just finish our chores early and call it a day. My head's all in a spin, and I need time to think."

Aimee nodded in agreeance, and silently walked away to Monnie's paddock, tears streaming down her cheeks. Her breath locked in her throat, choking her; she wouldn't let Sarah see her like this — that would be unfair. She knew how hard Sarah worked to pay off Trailblazers and her financial situation wasn't good, and her living there as well made life even more complicated and expensive. Selling Monnie would make life considerably more comfortable for her. All this logic ran through her head, breaking her heart.

Monnie stood at the gate, waiting for her, and nuzzled her neck as she opened the gate. It was more than Aimee could cope with and she buried her loud, uncontrollable sobs into Monnie's shiny black neck then wandered to the far end of the field, Monnie following her like an obedient puppy, as she found a place to let her grief pour out without Sarah hearing, a place she could stay until she had no more tears left to cry.

By the time she returned to the stables to bed Monnie down, Sarah had already completed the chores and had returned to the house. She looked up as Aimee came in, and Aimee tried to smile, but it didn't work, and she knew her tears were obvious. She washed her face in the bathroom and pushed down the lump in her throat that had been making it hard to breathe, and hard to control her thoughts. Sarah had their meals on the table when she returned and she sat and stared at her plate, still trying to hide her red eyes. Sarah sat opposite her and also stared at her plate. The silence became torturous.

Finally, Aimee sniffed and wiped her nose on a tissue. Without looking up, she said, "I know you have to sell her. I accept that." Her tears started again.

Then she heard Sarah sob. "I'm sorry …"

Then silence reigned again, both fighting with the heartache that gripped them. Then Sarah drew a deep breath and let it out. She stopped poking at her food and laid her fork down, then looked across at Aimee. "I've been thinking so much my head hurts," she said, "and it keeps going around and around of what is most logical and what is the right thing to do in the long term."

Aimee kept staring at her plate, knowing what was coming, knowing Sarah had also been crying. She'd owned Monnie since she was a foal. And then she felt selfish that she had thought only about herself.

"Look, I've read the contract carefully and it is legitimate. It states that you will ride Monnie in the Nationals – it does allow you to fulfil your dream: you will ride at the Nationals."

Aimee nodded, acknowledging the comment and poked at her salad. She dared not try to speak.

"It won't be the end of your riding career … With what he is willing to pay for Monnie, we could afford to keep one or two of the babies. It might mean starting from scratch again, but you have the skills now to bring a baby all the way through to the top and go beyond the Nationals. You are good enough to do that, Aimee. I also have to consider that every day, and every ride, and every time we put Monnie on the float and drive out of here to a show, something could happen, and her career would be over. Horses hurt themselves so easily, maybe we have just been lucky up until now, and you would *still* have to school a new horse up through the ranks. I know it could take another five years or more, but you are young enough, Aimee … and I am still here to help you. Trailblazers will still be here."

Aimee let out a heavy breath. The logic boggled her brain. Everything Sarah had said was possible, and she'd silently had the same fears for Monnie every day, that one day she would be injured somehow and her career would be over – not just because of her dream, but because she loved Monnie with all her heart. That was the hardest part in all this: she loved Monnie, and she knew Monnie loved her, and that is why Monnie strived so hard to perform well … because Aimee had asked her to.

"I can see Monnie now, happily running around with a beautiful little foal at foot. Can you see it, Aimee? She is getting older now and maybe it is her time to be a mum."

Aimee could see it: her beautiful black mare grazing contentedly in a lush green paddock with a stunningly elegant black foal beside her. That would be the epitome of joy to see.

She poked a piece of chicken into her mouth and chewed with her head down. Then she poked another piece in. She wondered as she chewed if Louie would ever be good enough to rise up the levels, or Thor with his powerful exuberance. Regardless, she had to stay focused on competing at the Nationals, of not just competing, but winning – Monnie deserved to go out with the win – to be the champion mare she was.

Sarah pulled a tissue out of the box on the table and blew her nose as her tears started to flow again. "Please understand, Aimee. Please don't …"

Aimee sniffed as well, and also pulled another tissue out. "I do understand why you need to do this," she replied softly. "I don't …" but that was all she could say. She returned a smile to Sarah to acknowledge that she fully understood Sarah's predicament.

That night never seemed to end, Aimee lying awake dabbing at her tears and trying to smother her sobs, knowing in the morning Sarah would sign the contract and sell her beautiful

Monnie. Her focus now would be to enjoy every day she had with her.

Michael Truscott arrived at nine o'clock precisely, armed with a cheque for the specified amount. They exchanged contracts and sealed it with a handshake after Sarah added a further clause that Monnie would remain in her care until after the Nationals. He confirmed that Monnie's insurance would be upgraded to cover the sale price, which Sarah promptly attended to.

The Nationals were fast approaching and Aimee intensified Monnie's schooling to ensure she performed exceptionally well in their final competition, always ending with a barrage of hugs and kisses, knowing how hard their final days together would be. She was also surprised to note that Sarah had taken Louie and Thor off the market.

Chapter 27

Uneasy Feelings

Aimee found her mother sitting on a bench in the hostel garden when she arrived for her visit. It had been the same each time she had come in the months after her mother had been moved from the hospital into nursing care. Only now her mother looked more gaunt, the lines in her face sinking deeper. Her jaundiced skin indicated that her kidneys were not functioning as well as they should and she looked a lot older than her forty-two years. A cold shiver of fear ran up Aimee's spine.

Her mother just sat staring at the flowers, waiting to recommence the conversation about her coming home 'so she could take care of her daughter, like a good mother should'. Aimee prepared herself for the conversation, which they'd had every time she came.

"Hi, Mum, what are you doing out here today? Have you had your afternoon tea?" Aimee felt pleased that the sternness had left her mother's face when she saw her approaching.

"I'm out here for peace and quiet – too much dithering going on in there. I can't wait to get home to my quiet space. When are they going to let me out of here?" It was the same question, over and over, visit by visit, and Aimee prepared herself to give the same reply.

"I am well enough," Rachael went on. "They just want to keep me here under lock and key, watching, always watching …"

Yes, they are watching, Aimee thought but didn't say. She

understood her mother's frustration, but also knew the hostel's reasons for keeping her mother there: they needed to ensure she had lost the desire to use alcohol as a crutch. Her mother had not been able to resist asking for the crutch that had worsened her condition, and it was a never-ending rollercoaster of her being well, then not being well. She needed to be constantly watched for her mental state, watched to a degree that Aimee could not achieve. Aimee also knew that the next time she relapsed she may not be so lucky with her health, the considerable damage she'd done to her internal organs now irreversible.

She slid onto the seat beside her mother. "Now you need to remember, Mum, I am leaving for Perth to ride in the Nationals soon so I won't be around to keep an eye on you at home. I'll be away for at least three weeks."

A tear fell from her mother's eye. "I won't see you for three weeks? Oh, Aimee, how will I survive not seeing you for three weeks …"

"You'll survive, Mum. These lovely ladies here will look after you and I will ring you and let you know how I am doing."

Rachael squeezed her hand. "Of course. Of course, you will ring me. How silly of me. You will be riding in the Nationals. I am so proud of you, darling. You will do well; I know you will. And you will ring me when you win, won't you? And ring me even if you don't win, I will be proud of you anyway."

"Yes, Mum, I will ring you regardless." Aimee gave her a warm smile, and smiled inwardly. The conversation had turned. She sighed a breath of relief, then felt Rachael grip her hand. "And when you get back, we will get to do the house up and we will be together again." Her mother's eyes brightened, and her lips curved slightly upward. "You give Monnie a big kiss of luck for me."

"I will," Aimee promised, deciding at that moment not to tell her mother about Monnie's sale.

They sat quietly together for a while, occasionally remarking on the beauty of a flower, or a bee hovering over a leaf, Aimee feeling her mother's frailty. Eventually, she kissed her mother goodbye and left, a distinct, uneasy feeling creeping over her that she may not ever see her again. She pushed the thought instantly from her head. She was just being stupid: it was just because this was the first time she would be out of the state and not within thirty minutes of her mother's side.

Aimee stopped at the entrance to the hostel garden and looked back. Her mother was again staring blankly at the flowers.

A sudden urge struck her and she raced back to her mother with her arms opened wide. "I forgot to tell you how much I love you, and I expect you to be here waiting for me when I get back. Is that a deal?" Aimee's tears flowed instantly, which surprised her: she didn't think she had any tears left.

Prising herself away, she headed straight home and packed her personal equipment and the truckload of gear she would need for Monnie, double-checking she had everything she'd need.

Two days later, they floated Monnie to the Equestrian Centre, all booted up ready for the four-day journey across the Nullabor to the isolated city of Perth. She loaded onto the horse transport truck with relative ease and settled with the rest of the team's horses. Giving her a quick pat before the ramp was raised, Aimee and Sarah stood back and watched as the truck pulled out and disappeared into the distance.

"I feel like I've just lost my best friend," Aimee murmured sadly, suddenly realising it would feel a lot worse in two week's time when they would say goodbye to her forever.

"Me too," Sarah sighed. Then she nudged Aimee in the ribs.

"Chocolate?"

"You bet," Aimee agreed, needing their 'go-to' for all occasions happy or sad.

The following day Karen arrived to manage the centre in Sarah's absence, which she had often done while Sarah and Aimee were away competing. The babies were turned out to spell while Aimee was away, and booked lessons were kept to a minimum.

With Monnie already on her way, Aimee and Sarah concentrated on preparing for their flight to Perth, delivering all her tack and riding apparel to the team manager for special shipment and insurance.

The following day, in the airport lounge, Aimee fidgeted with nerves and excitement as she had never been on a plane before. Her pacing along the windows looking at the row of planes was soon broken by the airport PA system.

"Attention all passengers. Flight QF1003 for Perth is now boarding through Gate Three. Could all passengers on Flight QF1003 please make your way to the gate for boarding?"

"Sarah, is that us?"

"Yes, it is." Sarah smiled.

"Oh … my butterflies are coming with us," Aimee said as she queued with other members of the team and their family escorts.

"You all look very smart in your state jackets," Sarah said, her grin showing her pride in what each rider had achieved. Each rider stood out in their uniforms with the blue and red pocket badges.

"I just hope Monnie has settled," Aimee said to Sarah as she buckled her seatbelt for her first-ever flight. "This is the first time Monnie has been anywhere without us. I hope she doesn't feel rejected without all the attention she's used to getting." More so, she hoped she didn't hurt herself on the long trip over.

"Just be aware that she might be quite unsettled when she arrives. Trips like this can put some horses off their game — some might be stiff and sore, some might be sour," Sarah warned. "Monnie is easy to read so we will play it by ear when we get her back in our care."

Aimee enjoyed the four-hour flight, the window seat allowing her to look out at the vastness of land below, though at times cloud cover filled the window, and her thoughts frequently drifted to her life and how it would be after the Nationals. She thought about her mother and wished she could be there to watch her, and she wondered what it would be like when she returned and they would be together. Her head filled with thoughts in the hours of flying, and she was glad Sarah had immersed herself in movies, rather than wanting to talk about the competition, or Monnie. She just had to push the thoughts of losing Monnie out of her head and concentrate on the job she had come to do, the dream she had come to achieve. She and Monnie were going to be champions. This was her only chance to achieve it.

Landing in Perth, they were greeted by the president of the Western Australian Dressage committee. "Hello, Jeannie," she gushed to the team manager. "I'm Margaret Donavan, the event's coordinator. Welcome to Perth!"

She continued to talk as the group headed to the carousel to collect their luggage, Sarah and Aimee learning the logistical arrangement that had been made for the team, and very glad to hear that there had been no problems so far and everything was running smoothly. Jeannie advised everyone that the horses were travelling well and were due to arrive at Millfields Equestrian Complex the following day.

Outside, the Perth weather confronted them — hot, but not as humid as Sydney, and they all agreed it would take some getting used to. Then the bus Jeannie had organised to transport them to the stables and their accommodation arrived, both venues adjoining so riders would have easy access to their horses. Each team member murmured their appreciation of this.

For Aimee, the final dream was coming within her reach.

Chapter 28

Life Skills

Dinner that night was a noisy affair at a local restaurant, attended by all the competitors and their support crew. Local riders and the event committee mingled and exchanged stories about their past experiences. Aimee's butterflies diminished slightly when others admitted to also being nervous, and she soaked up every bit of information she could and stored it for that one day she would be able to use it to her benefit. This was paradise.

She and Sarah crawled into bed in the early hours of morning after revelling in the atmosphere and companionship: the seriousness of the competition would begin in three days. For now though, Aimee felt exhausted, yet excited as Monnie would arrive that afternoon. She needed to see her again and looked forward to working her in the new surroundings.

The facilities at Millfield's Equestrian Centre were far superior to Sarah's. The arena was larger and encased by a colourful hedge; the stable block was equipped with internal warm water wash bays, washing machines and piped music. This was a concept Aimee could get used to very quickly. But for now, she would focus on preparing everything for Monnie: a soft bed, fresh water laced with molasses to disguise the difference in water taste, and a good feed to settle her in.

Early in the afternoon, a large white Mack truck containing all the champions pulled into the yard and everyone stopped what they were doing to watch it maneuver around in the parking area. Riders and handlers from New South Wales immediately gathered to the front of the crowd, eagerly waiting for the ramps to come down. Aimee moved to the front, anxious to see the precious cargo within and receive Monnie into her hands again. Four days had been too long apart.

The first horse down the ramp was Tracy Bell's Superman, who stood erect, checking out the unfamiliar surroundings. Next, Helen Mount's big grey horse, High Tower, exited the truck with one enormous leap, almost pulling the handler off his feet. Helen's dad quickly took him in hand and marched him off down the asphalt out of the way. Immediately after was Isabelle Troop's Best Friend, who nickered on seeing her.

Aimee could hear Monnie whinnying inside the truck, her high-pitched call unmistakable. Had she sensed she was there, waiting. Then the last partition was drawn aside and Monnie appeared in the dark opening. She stopped, at first watching her companions moving away to the stable blocks, then she focused on the gathered crowd, searching. Aimee stepped forward to take her from the handler, Monnie immediately pulling her handler forward towards her. She rested her head on Aimee's chest and Aimee gave her the biggest hug in return.

"You didn't like that big long float ride, did you," Aimee whispered. The mare nuzzled closer in response. "Come on, let's get you settled." She clipped the lead rope onto Monnie's headcollar, and the handler removed hers.

"She'll be a bit unsteady on her feet for a while," the woman said. "It's quite normal after such a long ride."

Aimee nodded and thanked her, and together they walked Monnie to a grassed area near the arena, allowing her time to stretch her legs and regain her balance. Then the woman removed Monnie's leg boots and checked her over to ensure she had arrived in good condition.

"Her lower legs are a little puffy," she said, "but that's not unusual after a long trip, and she was okay at the last stop. The swelling should come down once she starts walking around."

By now Sarah had arrived and she nodded her agreement and Aimee breathed a sigh of relief. Sarah had done this, probably many times, before. She would know what to worry about.

Monnie was turned out into a small grassed enclosure to graze for a further half-hour, then was put in her stable to rest.

"We will need to take her out for regular walks," Sarah said as they leant over the stable door watching their precious mount. "She's not used to being stabled up for long periods of time during the day and she will need that exercise to keep the swelling down in her legs."

"Yes, I can do that," Aimee agreed.

"We can take turns," Sarah smiled. "We'll make a roster to take her out at regular intervals, and you can ride her out for long walks, alternating that with arena work."

"And tonight we'll give her a full massage."

"… and tonight we'll give her a full massage," Sarah agreed. They were both on the same wavelength – it was like her thoughts were Sarah's thoughts, and she wondered if that was what it was like to have a best friend.

After a buffet dinner, provided by the equestrian centre, Aimee and Sarah brushed Monnie vigorously to stimulate her circulation, then commenced a thorough deep massaging of her muscles, at the end of which they heard Monnie whuffling contentedly –this was the sign to leave her in peace. Sarah placed a light rug on her as Perth nights were not as cold as New South Wales, then they said goodnight to her, and adjourned to the dining room for a cup of hot Milo before retiring. Many other competitors had the same idea, but their raucous conversation soon had them escaping to their rooms – they'd had a long day and had a busy fortnight ahead of them.

Chapter 29

The Price to Pay

Buckets clanging and voices shouting early morning commands woke Aimee from a deep dream. Her eyes flew wide open, and she realised she had overslept and Monnie would be desperately waiting for her early morning escape from the stable and a nice tasty breakfast. She quickly changed clothes, knocked on Sarah's door then raced down to the stables to attend to her regal queen. Monnie's familiar whinny rang out down the corridor when she saw Aimee coming.

"I'm here, Your Majesty," she said, grabbing her headstall off the hook. She slipped it on and led Monnie out of the stables and around the complex to the lush grassed pen to graze. Then Sarah appeared with her grain feed, which Monnie tucked into ravenously before being led to the grassed area.

"At least she hasn't lost her appetite," they both said in unison, then smiled widely at each other.

While Aimee walked Monnie around the grounds, Sarah cleaned the stable, which had to be done three times a day. It was ready by the time Aimee returned with Monnie for her breakfast. Then Aimee and Sarah wandered up to have their own breakfast, which was similar to the previous day's.

"I could eat a horse," Aimee admitted, sliding onto the seat beside Sarah, who smiled at her.

"Go ahead. It's free."

Aimee sighed deeply. "I would, but I'm riding in four events.

If I keep eating like this, sooner or later the buttons will pop off my jacket … in the middle of my test!"

Sarah grinned. "You can eat half a horse," she said. "Your allocated arena time is mid-afternoon and Monnie will need another walk before then so you will walk off what you eat."

In the mid-afternoon, Aimee saddled Monnie as usual and rode her to the arena, noting that a number of competitors were standing about watching. She felt like a fish in a fishbowl but also knew that there wasn't any option other than to perform to her best. Straight away, she felt Monnie's stiffness, and hoped it was only from the long float journey from home. She worked her through stretching exercises, then contracting exercises, blocking out the crowd that swelled to a larger audience nearby. She noticed Sarah give her the thumbs up, and swung Monnie into some lateral movements, little by little feeling the subtleness returning beneath her. Each circuit of the arena, she noticed more people watching, heard some cameras click, the whole experience unnerving her. Usually, she only had to perform for the judges. She tried to release her breath, which she realised her nerves had trapped in her lungs, and let out a loud exhale. Then she sat more erect, blocked the crowd from her mind and randomly rode the movements of all four tests, hoping she would remember them in the right order when the time came. Then she put that thought out of her mind. She only had one test per day, so now she only had to remember that first test, which simplified things.

As she rode, Aimee had noticed out of the corner of her eye a tall elegant lady, who appeared to be accompanied by an even taller good-looking man. She knew they were just part of the crowd, but the way they kept looking at Monnie made Aimee wonder why they observed her so intently, and because of this she couldn't blot them out of her vision. They just stayed there in sharp focus each time she looked up, and they continued to watch even after she started to cool Monnie down. They didn't depart until Monnie was securely back in her stable. They then disappeared like magic, only to reappear at the beginning of Aimee's first test. Aimee had discussed this with Sarah, who'd dismissed it as "Just admirers."

Two days later, the whole team was transported to the Equestrian Centre, affectionately known as Cravenhood, a huge venue with an indoor arena, surrounded by wide open fields surrounded by natural bushland. The large open fields now contained three arenas, marked out superbly with white-railed borders, splashes of vividly coloured flowers in tall white boxes that contained the arena markers, and pristine yellow sand as the base for all arenas. Covered grandstands flanked the main field, positioned to ensure a great view of the competition, and wood-chipped warm-up arenas were screened by rows of trees and white flowering hedges. All across the venue, competitors walked in spotless jodphurs and tailored jackets worthy of any Olympic event. Many grooms wore shirts with colourful emblems, promoting their riding centre, or rider. With all the excitement around her, Aimee's butterflies doubled in size and quantity and, even after many deep breaths, they remained swimming in her stomach, determined to stay.

She fussed about checking Monnie's bridle, doubly ensuring the chain sat flat in the rings of the double bridle, wiped off non-existent smudges on her boots. It was now her moment of glory; time to show the world what she had worked so hard for – time to make her mother proud. Aimee entered the warmup area and prepared Monnie for her first test. After fifteen minutes, the PA system broke through her thoughts, calling her for gear checking. She was still amazed that at this level they still checked before each event.

"Aimee Gardiner on Monique," the gear checker announced. Aimee nudged Monnie forward and waited while he proceeded to check Aimee's gear thoroughly. After ticking Aimee's name off on the sheet, he gave the usual instruction to go to the end of the arena and wait; she would compete after No. 26, and he pointed to the big grey horse in the distance.

Aimee took several deep breaths and uttered a few comforting words to Monnie, hoping that she would not disgrace herself amongst such brilliant talent. She also wanted to ride the best test she had ever done so this would be the best memory of her career with Monnie. Then she muttered under her breath, "This is for you, Mum."

In almost no time, she was summoned to commence her test, riding in front of an enormous crowd, this time, sadly, her mother not one of them.

As she sent Monnie into a trot on a line down the outside of the arena, she noticed the elegant lady and tall gentleman standing just behind the barriers and a shiver raced up her spine. *They're back* tore through her mind, blocking out the test. Her chest tightened instantly.

Then Sarah's voice in her head overrode her thoughts. That quiet voice of calm instruction: 'Block everything else out, Aimee. Breathe. Focus. Breathe … and visualise. You are a champion. Ride like a champion.'

Aimee let out her breath and drew a full deep breath back in as she reached the other end of the arena. Then she subtly rolled her head to loosen her neck and shoulders. Sitting taller in the saddle, she made her grand entrance through the A markers at canter. After an astounding square halt right over X, Aimee breathed in and out, pulling the focus fully back in, then respectfully saluted the judges. They nodded back, indicating they were ready for her to show them her quality of movement and elegance. Monnie responded instantly to her aids, as if she also knew she had to do her best test ever. They trotted forward in full collection into the first movement: a circle at B.

Aimee knew her halt would have earned high marks and she strived to perform the remainder of the test with equal precision. Her flying changes were exact and rhythmic; her walk half-pirouettes immaculate. *So far so good*, she thought. The competition was the stiffest she'd come up against and she knew she could not afford her extended trots across the diagonal to let her down, as they had done a few times before. This was a hard movement as she was never quite sure how much she could push Monnie without her breaking into a canter. This time she allowed Monnie to find her own ground, making sure she maintained her rhythm in the saddle to allow her to stretch her stride to the fullest. Fortunately, they too felt faultless and now she was gathered back in hand to execute the final canter to X.

Aimee kept her leg pressure equal down the centre line, keeping Monnie straight; she focused fully on the judges, then noticed the elegant lady watching Monnie and smiling. She closed her legs on Monnie's side, asking for a nice square halt, but instead got a very abrupt halt that was not square, Monnie more responsive than she'd anticipated. She reprimanded herself for being distracted, and composed herself enough to execute a neat salute to the judge.

She would have lost marks for the mistake but hoped the remainder of the test would be enough to get her into the placings. She had to wait until the remaining five competitors had completed their tests to see just how badly she had faired with that error.

She returned to the stables and put Monnie away, anxiously awaiting the results yet furious with herself for losing focus. She'd let other concerns infiltrate her first priority.

The class eventually finished, and the PA called all the riders back to the arena for the announcement of the results. Aimee remounted Monnie, gave Sarah a big hug, murmuring, "I'm sorry … I mucked it up," and trotted into the presentation area with the other competitors.

"Ladies and Gentlemen, we have the results of the Intermediare II dressage test, and what a very close competition it was," the official said, "a very close competition indeed." Then the formal speeches and words from the sponsors followed, and then …

"I will now announce the winners. In first place is Susan Mansfield from Western Australia on Dream Team.

The crowd erupted with thunderous applause and cheers, and the announcer waited until the noise died down.

"In second place is Sonya Harrigan from Tasmania on Toy Boy." The crowd erupted again, but soon fell silent waiting for the remaining results.

"In third place is Aimee Gardiner from New South Wales on Monique."

Aimee's eyes quickly welled with tears, and the dryness in her throat dissipated. She was in the top three. She had hoped for such a result but had not expected it, and noticed Sarah's eyes were glistening too.

The remaining three places were called out but she didn't hear them, just continued to pat Monnie with elation as the sashes were presented to each of the placegetters.

Then she fell into line for the traditional lap of honour around the arena, each rider smiling broadly. Aimee could have continued doing laps, as she'd never felt prouder. She'd finally achieved one of the most important tests of her career, but she left the arena with the others so the next class could begin their riding dreams.

Back at the stables, Aimee unsaddled Monnie with Sarah's help, Aimee too excited to focus on anything she was doing. Eventually, Sarah told her to go and sit on a chair and admire her sash. Smiling, Aimee obeyed and soon a crowd of well-wishers gathered to congratulate her and pat Monnie over the stall gate.

Then Aimee borrowed Sarah's mobile phone and rang her mother.

"Hi, Mum. How are you?" Aimee asked loudly, trying to be heard above the noise around her.

"Oh, darling, I am glad to hear your voice. I assume you got there okay. How is Perth?" Rachael asked more random questions before Aimee could get a word in.

"Mum, I'm fine. I got third in my first test. I just wanted to let you know."

"Oh, darling, I have been wondering how it was going over there. I am sorry I can't be with you. That is fantastic news. Is Sarah pleased?"

"Yes. Yes, she's more thrilled than I am. Mum ... are you okay?"Aimee squeezed the question in, noting the dull tone of her mother's voice.

"Yes, I'm fine, dear. Just very tired at the moment. They're playing with my medication again, that's all. Now tell me all about your day."

Aimee described the atmosphere of the competition to her mum, constantly aware of the cost of the call and her mother's deteriorating voice. Her mother obviously needed to rest so she finished the call with an excuse that she was needed. Her mother wished Aimee good luck for the remaining tests and rang off.

Pleased that she had phoned her mother, yet now worried by it, Aimee joined Sarah to prepare Monnie for the trip back to Millfields, and to prepare for the next day.

With the first test over, Aimee focused on the next event, and began to feel more confident about performing – she just had to blot out any distractions – any distraction at all. *Breath, focus, visualise*, she chanted throughout the rest of the day. *Just think about tomorrow's test.* For now though, she needed rest.

With Monnie loaded into the truck, they returned to Millfields, only fifteen minutes away. Monnie was comfortably bedded down and enjoying a grain-laced feed, so Sarah and Aimee joined their colleagues in the dining room for a quick dinner, a warm cup of Milo and a recount of the day before they retired for the night.

The next gruelling competition was only fifteen hours away.

Chapter 30

The Unexpected

Morning arrived sooner than expected, which it often did on competition days, but Aimee and Sarah were well organised as usual. After the short walk across to the stables to give Monnie her breakfast, Aimee noticed one of the competitors sitting on a chair outside her stable, sobbing. She hurried to her while Sarah went ahead to get Monnie's breakfast.

"Sue, what's wrong?" Aimee asked, fearing the worst.

Through the flood of tears, the girl said, "Magic got cast in the stable last night and has taken all the skin off her knees, and she's exhausted herself trying to get up. She looks terrible."

This was a nightmare Aimee had always feared as it could happen to any horse at any time. She glanced over the stable door to see Sue's beautiful bay mare standing very sedated, its head lowered, and wads of padding and bandages around both knees.

Aimee placed her arms around Sue's shoulders. "She's going to be alright, isn't she, Sue? She will be alright, won't she?"

Sue's tears flowed again, and she slightly shook her head. "We don't know. The vet said time will tell. But she's out of this competition, and maybe out for a long, long time. I just want her to be okay."

"Me too," Aimee said, her own vision blurring as a lump rose in her throat. They sat silent for a while, then Sue's father returned and Aimee slipped away to check on Monnie.

"That's so tragic," she said to Sarah as they prepared Monnie for the truck ride back to the State Equestrian Centre. "What an awful way to end a career."

Sarah simply nodded and sighed deeply.

As the truck ramp raised, sealing Monnie in, Sue waved Aimee goodbye and wished her luck.

Time pushed at them that day. Aimee brushed Monnie thoroughly, while Sarah tightly plaited her mane and tail, completing the task of making Monnie look magnificent. Aimee then rushed to the changerooms to don her breeches, shirt, stock and jacket. Sarah was dusting off her helmet when she returned, and had a damp cloth ready to dust off her shiny black boots once she was in the saddle.

With just under an hour to go Aimee sat quietly on a chair outside the stable, mentally going through the movements of the test before mounting Monnie for her grand performance. Just the thought of heading for the markers at A sent Aimee's butterflies soaring, and in this event they were performing loop-the-loops.

Heaving a deep breath as Sarah led Monnie out to her, she pushed the butterflies into stillness with 'Focus and breathe.'

'You can do this.'

'Ride like a champion.'

She smiled as Sarah offered her hands to bunk her into the saddle. "Are you ready for this?" Sarah asked before she hoisted her up.

Aimee gathered up her reins and took hold of the saddle. "I'm ready." Then she was up there, in the saddle, her reins set and balls of her feet set lightly on the stirrups. "I am definitely ready."

Sarah handed up her gloves, which Aimee pulled on firmly. Then she looked down at Sarah and half smiled with growing confidence.

"Ride like a champion," Sarah said.

"Ride like a champion," Aimee repeated, then she nudged Monnie forward towards the warm-up arena.

With fewer competitors this day, Aimee soon noticed the distinctive couple from the previous day watching her again. She tried to push them from her vision, concentrated on riding the more difficult movements she had to perform in this test.

"Aimee Gardiner on Monique, report to the gear checker," broke her train of thought and she quickly composed herself and headed in that direction. The process was smooth and quick and soon enough she was waiting for the signal to enter the arena.

Although Aimee had now performed this test many times, she always lived in fear she would get the tests mixed up and accidentally execute a wrong movement as they were all very similar. Fortunately, she had not done that for a long time and she had mentally gone through this test in her head many times.

Before long she found herself riding down the outside of the arena towards the A end, ready to complete the test, a test involving the complicated movements of passage, single time flying changes at the canter, canter to halt transitions and piaffe. The slightest fault would deduct many marks from the final score, so Aimee had to concentrate throughout the entire test.

The familiar barp of a horn summoned her to commence.

She began her test as accurately as she had always done, building Monnie's energy as she headed down the long side outside the arena, bending her on a true curve to line up the centre of the A markers. "Go like a champion," she murmured to Monnie as they passed through the opening at A and executed a perfectly straight line down the centre line to X. She saluted with crisp preciseness then continued her test with all the elegance and grace of ballroom waltz.

The test swam through her head, like choreographed ballet,

each heart-pounding second feeling like the final minutes of a vital exam. Knowing she had high scores in her pocket, she rounded the corner and prepared Monnie for the extended trot across the diagonal line then sent her on. Monnie, floating along the straight line from M to K, stretched her trot to the maximum with no indication of breaking stride. Aimee tried not to smile – everything was perfect …

Then it happened.

As she prepared to gather Monnie back on the approach to K, Monnie's head flew up and she pricked her ears; stared straight at a cluster of yellow and red balloons hovering above the ground at the edge of the arena, bouncing her way. Many horses skittered away from other balloons that floated or bounced across the field, obviously having escaped from the display further over. Some riders were dislodged from the saddle and chaos enveloped the warm-up arena as several horses ran loose. It all happened so fast.

Focusing back on Monnie, Aimee realised she had strengthened and locked her neck. She tried to shake her off the bit to soften her down, but too late. Monnie leapt sideways, away from the frightening objects, and clattered through the white railing boundary. She only just managed to contain her between her hands and legs to stop her from bolting away, and brought her back under control as a slight breeze lifted the balloons and sent them higher, up over the nearby trees. Aimee quickly turned Monnie onto a circle and began to reassure her, settled her down and breathed with relief that it was over. Then she looked up, and her heart sank. She was outside the arena. An automatic disqualification.

She looked at the judges' box, hoping she would be given a reprieve because of the circumstances, but there was no sign of hope, and while the commentator was sympathetic to her plight, it did not alter the end result.

Her heart plummeting, she saluted the judges as a mark of respect and headed back to the stables, trying desperately not break down and cry in front of people. But a crowd had gathered in front of Monnie's stable, so she diverted to the warm-up arena, needing to regain her composure and help Monnie regain her confidence in the surroundings before the next test.

Only when the crowd at Monnie's stable dissipated did she return and unsaddle, hoping above all hopes that Monnie's confidence had not been completely shattered. She would not know that until she was back in the arena the following day.

She prepared Monnie for floating back to Millfields by taking her for a long walk around the grounds, returning only when the truck arrived to return them to Millfields.

She had decided in that time that this was probably not the sort of news her mother needed to hear.

Any chance of achieving her dream had now drifted further away. Dinner that night was a sombre affair, and she soon bid Sarah goodnight and retired early, mentally steeling herself for another attempt tomorrow.

Chapter 31

Dreams Can Come True

Monnie didn't seem affected by the ordeal the following morning and devoured her breakfast as she had done every other day. While she ate happily, Aimee and Sarah sat down to their own packaged breakfast and discussed the logistics for the day. They would catch the ten o'clock transport to Cravenhood, giving them plenty of time to prepare Monnie for the three o'clock test. That would also give Aimee time to walk Monnie around the grounds to help restore her confidence.

After half an hour of casually riding Monnie around, Aimee declared that she seemed unperturbed by the incident and continued to focus on the task at hand. She sighed with great relief, feeling Monnie would be okay.

Then she helped Sarah plait Monnie up for her test while Monnie whuffled contentedly at the attention.

Gossip drifted around the stables about the incident the previous day, and complaints had been lodged by others, but she felt pleased no harsh words were spoken to her about it. She had to keep looking forward, not back.

Monnie warmed up beautifully as usual and Aimee felt she once again had control of the situation as she worked her on circles and straight lines to soften her forehand and engage her hindquarters. She had just started working on her laterals when she hear her name called, much earlier than expected. She checked her watch for the time which confirmed she had another fifteen minutes before her scheduled gear check. The gear checker apologised but explained there had been two scratchings and they didn't want to hold up the rest of the class by waiting. Aimee reluctantly agreed to co-operate and compete early, wanting to get the test over and done with instead of waiting around.

She made her way down to the entrance of the arena as soon as the car horn indicated she could start. She quickly found herself halted at X and saluting the judges.

Monnie performed every movement admirably, perfect executions from what Aimee felt happening beneath her. The extended trot floated with power and ease and Aimee graciously picked her up into a lively collected canter, relieved that this time she stayed in the arena. Her single time changes of lead in the canter felt rhythmical and even, Monnie's responsiveness instantaneous as usual. It was like riding by telepathy.

Before she knew it the test had finished, and she had halted at G smiling enormously at the judges. The return salute from the judge was just as obliging. Feeling relieved that the test had gone well, she exited the arena in preparation for her concluding gear check then dismounted and led Monnie back to the stables with Sarah by her side.

"I think that test deserves chocolate later on," Sarah suggested.

No sooner had she finished the sentence, than a voice from behind verified that request. Sarah and Aimee spun around, their mouths gaping open on finding Glen standing in front of them.

Sarah threw her arms around him and followed it up with a huge kiss. "What are you doing here?" she asked brightly.

"I haven't seen Perth before so thought I'd pop over and have a look for myself. By the way, Aimee, that was a brilliant test. I was very proud of you."

With only five riders to go after Aimee, they kept Monnie

saddled for the presentation, and did not have long to wait before the PA requested all riders to return to the arena.

Aimee donned her gloves, accepted Glen's leg up into the saddle, pushed her helmet down on her head and rode out quietly to receive the results, Glen and Sarah walking hand in hand behind her. Sarah crossed her fingers and wished Aimee luck as she headed away from them.

The preliminary announcement was underway when all of the riders finished lining up in front of the judges' box.

"In first place, with an outstanding score of 72 per cent, is Aimee Gardiner on Monique."

Aimee could not contain the tears that welled up in her eyes. Sarah's eyes glistened the same until Glen, without looking at her, handed her his handkerchief.

"In second place, Tracy Bell on Lieutenant Commander. In third place is Helen Mount on High Tower … In fourth place is Jennifer Balding on Just Luck.

"Quiet, please. We still have a couple more … Fifth place goes to Sonya Beagley on Sizzling Lady, and in sixth place is Sonya Brown on Master Valentino.

"Congratulations to all of you."

Aimee was presented with a very decorative sash and a trophy, and Monnie now wore a triple-layered royal blue rosette on her browband. Aimee knew she would cherish these for the rest of her life.

"All right, a lap of honour, ladies, if you would please."

Glancing around to ensure each rider was ready, she set Monnie off into a loping collected canter, trying to keep hold of the trophy in her arms. Even the photographers frenetically snapping shots with their cameras couldn't diminish the smile or the tears pouring down her face. This was the best dream she could ever have wished for. Sarah and Glen raced over to the end of the arena to greet her as she rode out for the second last time.

"Dinner is on me tonight," Glen said as they packed Monnie's saddle away in the locked cage. "I think we all deserve a big celebration after that performance."

Aimee, still smiling that Glen had come so far to be with them, nevertheless declined the offer – they didn't need her tagging along everywhere. Instead, she opted to stay at Millfields for the celebrations being held in the dining room to commemorate the last night before the competition finished, and everybody returned to their various states of origin.

With Glen and Sarah not there, Aimee mingled, and enjoyed the compliments she received on her and Monnie's performance, and commiserations on the incident the day before.

"When you bounce back," a boy from Tasmania said to her, laughing, "you really bounce back, don't you!" Everyone in the group laughed. Then Aimee noticed an elderly lady sitting alone by the fireplace, enjoying a cup of tea with her biscuit. The lady sat quietly watching the dynamics of the crowd but did not appear too perturbed about being by herself. Aimee observed her for ten minutes before deciding to introduce herself and give her some company so she wouldn't be alone.

She broke the ice by asking, "Are you from Western Australia?"

"No. I am from Victoria," the lady said precisely. "I am the coach for the Victorian team. Shelia Watson."

Aimee's eyes lit up. This lady was legendary in the dressage fraternity, with many international successes to her name.

"It is a pleasure to meet you. My name is Aimee Gardiner."

"Yes, I know who you are, dear. I have been watching you throughout the competition and I think you have huge potential. You have a very special horse there as well."

"Thank you very much," Aimee replied.

They discussed the previous day's competition, how well the event had been organised, for the horses, the riders and the support crews, and agreed it was a credit to the organisers.

"Well, the next Nationals will be held in Victoria, so we had better shape up to be as good as these ones." Then she paused for a moment. "Aimee, what are your plans for the next few years?"

"I'm not sure really," Aimee admitted. "Monnie has been sold and goes to new owners after this competition so I will be starting again on a new horse when I get home, I guess."

"I had heard on the grapevine that she'd been sold, but didn't know if it was true." Shelia nodded to herself. "Someone has got themselves a very good horse. Do you know who the buyer is?"

"No, not yet. But we'll probably find out soon. All I know is that she was brought on someone's behalf, and I suspect they may have come to Perth for the competition."

"The reason I asked, dear, is …I was wondering if you would like to come and work for me at my stables in Victoria. You would be my head rider," Shelia said.

Aimee only just managed to stop her jaw from dropping. "I am extremely flattered," she said, thinking about Sarah, thinking about her mother, who she would need to phone soon. "I'm unable to take you up on the offer at this stage though. My mum's not well at the moment, but I'd certainly like to consider your offer at a later stage."

Conversation then turned to her mother, and Aimee was careful not to disclose the reason for her illness, and Shelia empathised with her situation.

"My offer will always stand," she said as she handed Aimee a business card. "It's been really nice talking to you, Aimee, and I am very honoured to have finally met you in person, but please excuse me for now as I have a long day ahead tomorrow and am looking forward to crawling into bed."

Aimee bid her good night and sat by the fire staring at her card and thinking what a wonderful opportunity it would be to ride for such a knowledgeable professional. But Aimee still had loyalty to Sarah, and also knew that with her mum the way she was, it simply wasn't feasible.

Chapter 32

The Spirit of the Dream

The next morning, Aimee woke at her usual time. Straight away, she noticed Sarah had not returned from her date or had simply slept through the loud knocking on the door. Accepting that Sarah was a grown lady, who seemed very happy with Glen, and they seemed to enjoy each other's company immensely, she continued on to the dining room for a token breakfast. She even baulked at the toast and decided on just a cup of Milo. Then she returned to her room, collected her clean clothes for the day's event and anything else she needed, and had them ready for the truck trip to Cravenhood for the last time.

She made her way to the stables to feed Monnie her long-awaited breakfast, the mare's shrill whinny greeting her forty metres from the stable. She'd seen her coming. She noted as she passed that Magic's stable was empty, and shuddered.

"Good morning, my beautiful champion," she greeted Monnie. "Well ..." She felt the familiar lump start to block her throat. "... this is your last competition today, so I hope you will do me proud ... just like yesterday." Tears now rose and poured onto her cheeks. She wiped them away, undid the stable door bolt and poured the feed into the appropriate bin then stood back and watched her eating as she recomposed herself. A flutter of different thoughts pushed their way in. "This is our last competition. This is the last breakfast I might be able to give you."

She patted Monnie's neck and her eyes again filled with tears. *This is for the best,* she told herself, knowing this might be her very last ride on Monnie. She prayed that her new owners were kind.

Determined that this was one routine she was not going to miss and, as there was still no sign of Sarah, Aimee decided to go on ahead and catch up with Sarah at Cravenhood. She loaded her big black friend onto the truck. Monnie gave her a reluctant look before consenting to Aimee's request to move into the bay she would occupy.

"You'll get a well-deserved holiday after all this is over, Monnie," she promised.

Arriving at the grounds, she was greeted by a blurry-eyed Sarah and Glen, who, judging by the smile on their faces, had had an enjoyable night.

"Looks like you two had a great night," Aimee noted with a raised eyebrow.

"Oh, we did," Sarah retorted. "We had a great night. I'll tell you about it later, but for now, let's get Monnie ready for her event."

Glen fetched the gear from the truck while Sarah began the morning ritual of dividing up the mane for plaiting. Aimee brushed and braided the tail while Monnie enjoyed a hay net full of sweet-smelling oaten hay.

With two experts on the job, it didn't take long for Monnie to look as glamorous as she had on every other day.

With only two hours to go before her final test, Aimee sat and watched some of the other tests in the arenas around the grounds, a luxury she hadn't allowed herself in previous days. She found this quite relaxing and felt more inspired to do well in her own test.

Eventually, she wandered back to the stables, returning the greetings of other riders who called to her by name as she passed. Many people seemed to know her now, which surprised her, and she responded, calling them by name also. She really now felt she was part of a close-knit group.

In the changerooms, she donned her elegant riding attire, which she was always proud to wear, and returned to the stables where Sarah had saddled Monnie and was waiting for her. Glen legged her up into the saddle and walked with her to the warm-up arena, feeling the starker heat of the approaching summer beaming down on her.

As this was the last day of the competition, and all tests were at the top level, many of the previous horses remained in the stables, which meant the warm-up arena was not as crowded as usual, and Aimee took advantage of the space. Monnie, however, indicated that she'd had enough, yet still performed admirably and Aimee hoped she would continue her willingness throughout the test. This was not the time to perform like a sour horse.

"Did you hear that, Monnie? This is not the time to behave like a sour horse. Today we have to shine," Aimee explained as she gave Monnie a reassuring pat.

Monnie's ear twitched back at her.

Just like every time before, she was called to go to the gear checkers – the usual ritual ensued: 'Be ready to enter on the horn.'

Aimee left the gear checking area and headed towards the arena, noticing instantly the familiar couple standing at the entrance of the grandstand; they were looking and pointing at Monnie. At that moment she wondered if they were the new owners and if they were waiting for the end of the competition before announcing themselves and taking Monnie from her. She forced the idea away. She would find out soon enough. Right now, she had a job to do. *Breathe. Visualise. Focus.*

She saw Sarah on the sidelines pulling out her phone and answering it. Sarah frowned, looked shocked. Aimee had now ridden past her; she looked back. Sarah looked suddenly stressed and had gripped Glen's arm.

Aimee rode a tight circle, watching her. The car horn blasted. Sarah forced a smile and gave her the thumbs up, yet tears rolled down her face.

Thumbs up. It's okay, Aimee thought. *It's all okay. Now focus! Breathe. Ride like a champion.* She gathered Monnie up beneath her, sat deep and rocked back to send Monnie into canter. They swung onto the curved line that would send them straight down the centre line. "Mum, this one's for you," she murmured as she lifted her spirits and passed between the markers at A.

From that moment, Aimee's vision centred. She was riding like a champion, and she was riding a champion. Every finger movement she made, Monnie responded to impeccably. It was like holding liquid gold in her hands. The test played out like a movie in front of her as she moved Monnie through passage to piaffe, to passage, to half passes across the arena and back again. The extended trot was like riding air, with Monnie's feet lightly touching the ground and all Aimee could think was … *This is for you, Mum.*

In the three-quarter line pirouette, she felt like a ballerina spinning on her toe point, precise, balanced, effortless, and reinback was a moment to breathe and rebalance, and count the steps precisely. In the final turn down the centre line, Aimee felt the immense engagement of Monnie's hindquarters lifting her stride through the final passage, complete elevation, to complete restrain in the piaffe – twelve elevated steps on the spot – and a fully grounded halt. Aimee couldn't help grinning. The movie had finished. She had ridden everything she had visualised. And now it was over. She felt the elation rise up in her chest.

Mum, we did it. We did it, Mum, the best we could.

She noticed the judges smiling at her, and remembered she hadn't saluted, and did so with respect and elegance. Then she breathed out fully and released Monnie's forehand to leave the arena in a completely relaxed manner. Sound then filled her ears. Loud sounds. She was back outside the arena, back in the real world. The crowd had risen to its feet. Cheers erupted from the stands; spectators shouted out to her and clapped vigorously. The familiar couple were no longer there. Sarah was no longer on the sidelines.

Patting Monnie with adoration and thanks, she headed straight for the stables. She couldn't believe it. Her final test was over and she had obviously impressed. She hoped the judges felt the same.

Tears rose to her eyes as she rode. Was this what it was like to be a champion? If it was, it was enough. She didn't care about scores; she had done what she had dreamed of doing. She had ridden like a champion; she had felt like a champion.

The crowd settled as she left the area, only competitors complimenting her on her test as she passed by them. She graciously said 'thank you' and she went in search of Sarah.

She found Glen at the entrance to the stables. He tried to smile but couldn't make it happen. He took hold of Monnie as she dismounted. "Sarah's in there," he said, pointing to Monnie's stall.

As soon as she reached the opening, she knew something was terribly wrong. Sarah had been crying, and could barely hold back her sobs. She looked pale.

"Sarah, what is it? What's happened?" she asked, suspecting she had received some really bad news.

Sarah just looked at her, sadness engulfing her face.

"Oh, Aimee, I'm so sorry. I'm so, so sorry …"

"What is it?" Aimee insisted.

Sarah pulled her down to sit on a stool they often shared when working with Monnie. "Aimee, I had a call just as you were about to start your test."

Aimee nodded, wary. She'd sensed it had been bad news.

"Aimee, your mum passed away this morning. I am so, so sorry."

Aimee sat stunned, barely feeling Sarah's arms wrap around her, deeply hoping she hadn't heard what she thought she'd heard. But Sarah's distress brought reality to her. She had never seen Sarah so distraught.

"How?" she asked dully. "How did she die?"

"The doctor said her organs just gave out. They tried everything but couldn't save her."

Aimee sat silent.

A long fifteen minutes passed, her thoughts drifting through numbness, then guilt, to acceptance and back to numbness. It just wasn't fair. She was losing Monnie and now she had lost her mum. Yet she sat, letting logic try and force its way in. She'd sensed that her mother was terminal, yet she'd come here to ride. She'd come here to make her proud. The big photo in the cupboard prodded her – her mother was proud of her, and she hoped she had made her proud again.

The familiar sound of the PA calling competitors in the Grand Prix level to return to the arena for the presentation ceremony. She sat, momentarily void of feeling as the call repeated.

Sarah went to the stable doorway. "I'll lead Monnie out and give your apologies," she said softly. "You don't have to go out."

Then she was gone and Aimee felt a sudden warmth wash over her. She had ridden her heart out for her mother, and for Monnie, and Monnie had worked her heart out for her. She owed it to both of them to see this through to the end, win or no win.

"No," she called out to Sarah. "I'll go." Aimee appeared in the corridor, and Sarah stopped and waited for her then gave her the biggest hug. Then Glen appeared with Monnie and legged her up into the saddle.

Sarah slipped Aimee's feet into the stirrups and dusted her boots. "Ride like a champion," she said with a sad smile.

"Ride like a champion," Aimee repeated then she turned Monnie towards the arena and nudged her into a collected canter to join the other competitors. This was the finale, and, as Sarah had told her when they had discussed her pathway, life must go on.

"Ladies and gentlemen," the commentator summoned silence from the crowd. "I present to you the finalists in the Grand Prix dressage competition."

The riders all glanced at each other up and down the line, eager, excited, uncertain in some cases.

"But first, a few words from our event organisers and the event sponsors ..."

Everyone stood waiting, impatience growing as the customary speeches delayed the big announcement. Then finally ...

"And now for the big moment," the commentator drawled, keeping the crowd in suspense. "The winners are ...

"In first place ... ... Aimee Gardiner on Monique!"

Aimee's mouth dropped open and her breath left her. But only for a moment. Breathing in deeply, she suddenly felt the spirit of her mother looking down on her, smiling and clapping with joy. Tears again blurred her vision and streamed onto her cheeks, but this time they were tears of pride. She patted Monnie profusely and wiped them away.

"In second place – Judith Dodd on True Blue. In third place is Simon Hislop on James Bond. Well done, your scores were all above 80%. An amazing effort.

"In fourth place is Sonya Beagley on Sizzling Lady. In fifth place is Helen Mount on High Tower and in sixth place is

Tracey Bell on Lieutenant Commander.

"Congratulations to all of you. When you have all received your sashes, a lap of honour please," the commentator requested.

Once again, Aimee accepted a beautiful sash and a huge trophy, which she handed down to Sarah. She waited, feeling her mother watching over her as the other riders received their sashes, then she nudged Monnie off around the arena in a brisk, controlled canter, Monnie tossing her head with the joy of the moment even though Aimee was choking on a hard lump in her throat. She would have loved for her mother to see her ride just one more time.

After one lap, the cheering spectators urged them on for another, Aimee thinking, 'if only they knew ....' But she also realised they did not need to know.

For the next half hour, she endured the attention of endless photos, journalist and television interviews, all the while wanting to get away, to hug Monnie in private time then to get back home. She hoped they excused the redness of her eyes as tears of joy while her heart thudded dully at what would come next. Feeling like her face had a permanent ceramic smile, she finally had a reprieve when the winners of the next event arrived for their presentations. Aimee sighed with relief. Dismounting from Monnie, she led her champion mare back to the stables for some well-deserved attention.

But the day wasn't over.

The familiar couple who'd been watching Monnie over the past few days stood waiting near her stall.

"Hello, Aimee," the elegant lady said.

"Hello," Aimee responded, feeling the tears rising again as she suspected what was coming next.

"My name is Audrey Hill. We are Monnie's new owners. May I please be the first to congratulate you on your tremendous riding and your wonderful successes over the past four days."

Aimee smiled and responded with a firm handshake. Her assumption had been right. "You will like her. She's a fabulous horse." She tried to sound business-like. This was not the time to express her emotions. They were too raw right now. "Do you live in Perth?" she asked.

"Yes, we do. We own a large stable complex in Darlingsong. Monnie will have the best of care and facilities, and please be assured that she will be well looked after."

"I don't doubt that," Aimee said, hoping it didn't come out the wrong way.

The couple chatted about Monnie and how they had watched her rise through the ranks, the conversation ongoing while Aimee unsaddled, unplaited and brushed Monnie down for the last time.

Then Audrey said, "We've brought the float and would like to take Monnie home today and get her settled in and we were hoping you would come up so you can see that she'll be safe and well cared for. We live not far from here."

Aimee's skin suddenly chilled that all this planning had been done without any consultation, but she also understood it was more logical to sever ties quickly. This would also allow her to fly home immediately without having to worry about her horse. As Glen and Sarah had mentioned they would like to stay on and do some sightseeing, she felt quite relieved that she'd not be inconveniencing anybody by going home so soon.

She noticed Sarah watching her intently; knew she would be worried at how she would take losing Monnie so quickly, on top of losing her mum. Aimee bit her lip to hold back her tears, then shrugged slightly. When Sarah saw her subtle nod, she knew her answer and nodded in agreement.

"My mum passed away this morning and I am flying home as soon as I can get a flight. It would be nice though to see Monnie settled before I go," she said quietly.

Audrey gasped. "Oh, I am so sorry. What an inconvenient time to be discussing such matters." A flush of heat struck Audrey's face and she looked as devastated as Aimee felt. "You poor child. You poor, poor child." She looked across at Sarah. "Yes, you simply must come up to Darlingsong. It will do Aimee good to see Monique settled in, and to help settle Monique in. Don't you think, Sarah?"

So Monnie was duly kitted out in a new silk tassled rug, and booted up for the trip to her new home. Aimee travelled with her in Audrey's enormous horse trailer, dwelling on how things happened for a reason: Monnie being sold to Perth owners meant she didn't have to worry about getting her back home and settling her back in while dealing with her mother's affairs. She felt a slight sense of relief at that. It was an apt excuse to cope.

Darlingsong was fifteen minutes from Millfields, so they had enough time to pack up Monnie's gear ready for the truck returning to Millfield, and then prepare Monnie for her trip to her new home.

Although Aimee enjoyed the drive up into the hills, and that she could say goodbye to Monnie in her new home, her thoughts dwelt sadly that she'd not been there to say goodbye to her mother. She should have been there and felt guilty that she wasn't. She had sensed this would happen on that last visit. Her mother had looked so ill, and she knew she shouldn't have gone.

Then an overwhelming feeling washed over her, a feeling that her mother was there, close by, with her in spirit. The feeling wrapping around her lifted her despair even though a tear rolled onto her cheek.

Arriving at the Darlingsong complex, Aimee, Sarah and Glen stood awestruck at the size of the complex. They knew their hometown had some very flash establishments, but this topped them all. The complex was set on fifty acres of lush green, irrigated pasture, with white, jarrah post and rail fencing. Each paddock had its own brick shelter, which was lined with fresh, clean, white sawdust. Audrey pulled up outside the enormous stable block and invited all three to look around while she unloaded Monnie and took her to the new paddock. Aimee followed Audrey to bid her last farewells to Monnie, trying hard to contain the tears that had welled up in her eyes again. She was also grateful for the tissues Sarah had slipped into her pocket earlier in anticipation.

To reach the adjoining paddocks they walked through the stable block, which consisted of thirty brick stables, also filled with fresh white sawdust. Inside the block were three wash bays with hot and cold running water, two washing machines, an indoor lunge arena as well as a rolling yard. Sarah's jaw was permanently open and Glen kept whistling with amazement at the height of elegance.

"Something to think about when you get home," he quipped to Sarah, but she just jabbed her elbow into his ribs and said, "As if …"

They then were outside the stable block, looking at a huge sixty metre by sixty metre indoor arena, with mirrors at the far end. Aimee and Sarah knew Monnie would certainly have the best of care, which made them feel more comfortable with their decision.

Audrey released Monnie into a huge paddock and watched her gallop around, exploring the perimeter of the new enclosure. After being locked up in a stable for nearly a week, she appreciated the run and the freedom. Monnie continued to frolic for a further few minutes then discovered the lovely green grass beneath her feet. Her head went down, and stayed down, and Aimee felt it was the right time to walk away.

She walked on ahead, pretending to go and look at the stable block, while she struggled with her loss. Away from the others, she snuck into an open stable to let the final flood of tears roll down her face, immediately cursing that she didn't have enough tissues in her pocket. Fighting back the next flow, she ducked back out into the sunshine while Sarah chatted with Audrey and her husband a short distance away. Finally, they moved on, finding Aimee sitting alone on a wall near the driveway and they all climbed back into Glen's hire car for the journey back to Millsfield. They bid Audrey and her husband farewell and thanked them for the tour, Sarah now more content with her decision, knowing Monnie would be well looked after for the rest of her life.

They returned to Millfields where Sarah helped Aimee book and pack for the flight home.

"I'm sorry, the earliest flight we can get you is in the morning. Glen and I are on the afternoon flight, that's the earliest one we could get on compassionate grounds. Karen will pick you up at the airport. Are you sure you will be alright?"

Aimee shoved her overalls and sneakers into her case. "I wish you and Glen would reconsider. You had planned to go sightseeing. Glen was looking forward to it."

"There's no way I'm going to let you go home alone to deal with this, and Glen doesn't want you to either. We can do this again one day ... maybe for our honeymoon ..."

Aimee stood up suddenly and looked at her.

"I was only kidding," Sarah said, smiling. "We can always do it another time. Right now, this is more important. Glen and I will get in about seven, and we'll get a taxi back. Karen will run you around and help where she can. I don't want you driving at this time. You'll not be thinking clearly. Do you hear me?"

"Yes, I hear you. You sound like my big sister."

Sarah smiled warmly then helped her toss more items into the case. "Glen will get you to the airport in the morning while I pack up everything for the truck and team manager to organise. You just look after yourself until I get there."

Then she hugged her tightly. "Just know I will be there as soon as I can."

It was all Aimee needed to help her through the night and early hours of the morning. She decided not to go to the dining room, knowing she would not be good company – she felt too physically and emotionally drained to deal with anything.

Chapter 33

Dreams Can Be Won

Aimee didn't sleep much that night, her mind continually running through a checklist of all the things she had to do once she arrived home. The first one would be to go and see her mother and bid her a proper farewell, even if it was only in body. She would worry about the other arrangements once that was done.

The morning passed quickly, everyone loading all their gear onto the truck ready for the trip to the airport; ensuring they left only the floating gear with the horses for the truck ride back to the east coast. Sarah bundled Monnie's in with their saddlery, her back to Aimee so it wouldn't set up any painful regrets. But Aimee had already noticed and let out a sigh that, while it was painful, there was nothing that could be done about it. As Sarah always said, "Life goes on."

Shoving her essential things into a small carry bag, Aimee prepared for her early flight, which would get her home a few hours earlier than the rest of the team. Glen drove her to the airport after everyone farewelled her with warm hugs and condolences. She knew she had made some wonderful friends and acquaintances over the past two weeks.

She boarded the plane and settled into her seat, feeling empty with Sarah not sitting beside her, but she would be with her soon enough, she realised, and smiled at the thought of seeing Sarah so happy with Glen.

Much to her surprise, she fell asleep an hour after takeoff and woke to the sound of the captain asking the crew to prepare for landing; she was grateful the flight had gone so quickly. Monnie and her mother had flitted in and out of her thoughts several times in her sleep – two great losses she would always remember this event, and year, for.

Karen's smiling face greeted her when she came through the terminal doors, a big block of chocolate waving in the air to cheer Aimee up. They hugged as tears started to well in Aimee's eyes again.

"I'm just grateful to be home," Aimee said as they piled into the car and began the journey back to Trailblazers, Karen drawing out an account of the competition and its adventures as she drove to keep Aimee's mind occupied.

Trailblazers now felt very empty without her two main buddies there, and Aimee gladly helped Karen feed the babies – now strapping, muscled two-year-olds – giving Thor and Louie a warm cuddle before heading back to the house. In the early afternoon, Karen drove her to the funeral home where her mother had been taken that morning. Details of the funeral and options were explained, which gave Aimee more things to think about. She wanted her mother laid to rest beside her grandmother, and knew now she was free of her misery – she had looked so serene – she had finally found peace. She felt sure Sarah would help her with some of the funeral decisions when she arrived home that evening.

Leaving that small decorative room grieving her loss, Aimee never felt so alone. Sarah wasn't there to share her grief; nor was Monnie. Soon she would have to consider where she would go from here. With Monnie gone, her dream fulfilled, and Sarah wrapped in Glen, it was certainly going to be a humungous 'Life goes on,' she mused. Life was going to change in a big way, and there was nothing she could do about it.

Returning to Trailblazers, she felt emotionally numb but prepared herself that, after the funeral in three days time, she would sort out her mother's affairs and continue on with her life, somehow. She eventually fell into a deep sleep, unaware that Sarah's and Glen's plane had just landed.

Early next morning at breakfast, Aimee offered to help Karen feed up, but Karen shook her head. "You need to be over at your mother's house this morning. That social worker who helped you before rang last night after you went to bed. She wants to meet you this morning and said your mother's house would be the best place."

"I'll drive you over," a voice came from behind Aimee. Aimee's head spun. *Sarah*! A warm pair of arms wrapped around her shoulders in a hug.

"How are you doing, sweetie? How was yesterday?"

Aimee hung her head, remembering. "I got through it," she said. "But I need to talk to you about some things … the funeral … and …"

"Finish your breakfast and we can talk on the way to your place," Sarah said, pouring herself a coffee.

Your place. Your place. Aimee realised at that moment that maybe her mother's house just might now be *her* place. Her Nanna had left it to her mum, and there was no one else to leave it to. Then she realised how sad that sounded. There was no one else but her left. She pushed her cereal around with her spoon. Now that also meant that, if she had a place, she would have to leave Sarah's.

A coldness rippled over her skin. She had lived her dream, but now her dream lifestyle was also coming to an end. She ran her hands deeply through her hair, clutched her head and heaved a deep sigh.

"You'll be fine," Sarah added calmly as she slid onto the seat beside her. "From experience, yes, things will be hectic for a while, but then … life goes on." She squeezed Aimee's hand. "You'll be fine. Now, finish your breakfast and I'll drop you off to meet with Theresa."

"No, it's okay. I can drive over. Could you instead sort things out with the funeral place?" … and that is what happened.

Driving towards her mother's house, even from a distance, Aimee could see it looked neglected – there'd not been any residents in it for some time.

Aimee parked in the driveway, and, opening the front door, immediately smelt the muskiness of isolation. The house seemed dead and suddenly felt very lonely.

She wandered through the rooms, remembering her mother's role in each of them, remembering the role she had played as she had grown and taken on more and more responsibility. She could not bring herself to enter her mother's bedroom though, not yet. Eventually, she stood in the lounge, pondering where to start and which direction should she take in pulling things back into shape. The mail had piled up on the side cupboard near the hallway, courtesy of the Carters next door, and she quickly flicked through them, with little interest – she would however have to deal with the letters soon. Then she remembered something and went to the cupboard containing the photo of her at the State Championships the year before. As she carefully removed it from its place, she noticed an inscription on the back. "To Aimee. Wishing you a happy, happy nineteenth. Love, Mum". That brought tears to her eyes. Her mother wouldn't be there for her nineteenth birthday. Nor would she be able to share the photo with her. She placed the photo on the mantlepiece above the fireplace, and stood back admiring how well it had been presented. She suddenly thought of Monnie and wondered how she was in her new home. Did she miss her not feeding her breakfast this morning? Would she even understand?

Refocus! Don't think! Life goes on …! she suddenly chided herself. With that, she started to open the mail, reluctant to see what disastrous surprises would confront her; wondering how she would ever pay the many outstanding bills she expected to find. She began prioritising the accounts that had to be paid soon from those that could wait a while when a knock came at the front door. Aimee quickly opened it to find Theresa Ward, the social worker, standing on the doorstep, right on time.

"Boy, am I glad to see you," Aimee admitted openly. "Please come in."

Theresa entered the lounge room and handed Aimee a tin of Milo and a litre of milk. "Here I figured these would come in handy … By the way, congratulations on your success in Perth," she continued.

"How did you know?" Aimee asked, surprised.

"It's my job to see that you are okay. I keep tabs."

Aimee went over and gave her a big hug. "Thank you. I need this."

"You're welcome. Now go put the kettle on and we will have a Milo and see what help you need in getting your mum's affairs in order."

After discussing the funeral arrangements over a hot cup of Milo, Theresa rose and rinsed her cup in the sink. Then she turned and said, "Your mum and I had a long chat when she realized how ill she was. She wanted to make sure you are well looked after. She told me she had a Deed box here somewhere which contains her will, which will direct you in the management of her estate." Theresa smiled thinly. "We just have to find that Deed box. Any ideas where it might be?"

Shrugging, Aimee looked up. "Most important stuff she keeps in her bedroom."

So the search began, every box and folder suitable to hold important documents flicked through, Aimee feeling guilty and uneasy going through her mother's things. In a drawer in one cabinet, they found folders with taxation forms and school reports, appliance warranties, medical records. Then, fossicking to the bottom of the drawer, Aimee found a thin folder that only contained a large orange envelope. She removed it from the folder and peeked into the envelope, then started pulling out the items one by one before reinvestigating the writing at the front of the envelope. There, Theresa stopped her; she put her finger firmly beneath the words Aimee now stared blankly at. In big capital letters was written ADOPTION PAPERS.

Aimee froze for a second frowning, then she gingerly pulled out more of the contents. There, on the bed in front of her lay the shock of her life. Her birth certificate, which she'd never seen before, and another certificate. Her heart began to thud, and her hands trembled at the heading on the paper: CERTIFICATE OF ADOPTION. Her hands covered her mouth as she looked up at Theresa. Then she read down the form.

The name on the top was Majorie Aimee Brown.

She read further.

Mother's name: Sarah Elisabeth Brown.

The adoption date was two months after Aimee's birthdate.

Aimee sank onto the bed, her legs feeling like jelly. Her mother had never mentioned any of this to her, let alone that Sarah was her real mother.

Theresa watched her, blinking with the realisation. "You didn't know about this?" she asked.

Aimee shook her head, too stunned for words. So much had changed in a few short moments, in the last two days. Now her whole life was a lie. She looked up at Theresa. "Why didn't she tell me?"

Theresa shook her head. "I don't know, honey. Maybe she

just wanted you to belong to her, and only her. That's what a lot of mothers do. Most mothers eventually bring it out in the open, some mothers just can't." She looked at Aimee intently. "Does it really make a difference? Really? She was your mother; she raised you, loved you ..."

Aimee still stared at the certificate, the words leaping out at her: Marjorie Aimee Brown.

Then Theresa broke her train of thought. "Look here, I found it," and she held up a document with 'Last Will and Testament" scrolled across the front. "Your mum's will." She handed it to Aimee to open and read.

As anticipated, all of Rachel's possessions were bequeathed to Aimee, and all monies held in the estate were for Aimee's future benefit. Theresa then went fossicking for any documentation of bank accounts so they could be legally transferred into Aimee's name. She soon found bank statements indicating there was not a massive amount of money available but enough to cover the outstanding bills, pay for the funeral, and keep Aimee financial for a short time. Thankfully, the house was freehold, paid out from her grandmother's estate.

Aimee heaved another deep sigh. Even with her mother's illness, she had been money-wise, and she loved her for that, on top of everything else. But her hand still lingered near the certificate in front of her.

"Do you think that was why she resented my riding at Sarah's — not at first, but later when she found out Sarah's surname. She was always on edge around Sarah, you know. Thinking about it, she always seemed nervous when Sarah and I were together." Aimee looked up. "Do you think she was scared that we would one day work it out? My birthday was Sarah's daughter's birthday. We look similar, have the same passion ... but we never connected it — and Sarah gave me such wonderful birthdays, like I was really special to her."

"You are special to her, honey. Not many ladies will take in a waif on the spur of the moment and look after you like she did, for all these years. That is connection. Maybe your mum did see it, and maybe she was scared, but she loved you like you were her own. She would never think any differently." Theresa sighed.

"Well, my girl, what a day this has been. Knowing what you know, what are you going to do now?"

Aimee slowly gathered the documents and certificates and slid them back into the envelope. One part of her wanted desperately to ring Sarah and break the news to her; the other part warned her it could change everything, ruin their relationship, and life was changing so rapidly right now she didn't want any more changes. "I really don't know," she said. "I really don't know. It's something I will have to sleep on."

Aimee did just that. She slept on it the first night. She slept on it the second night, albeit both nights tossing and turning over and over. The one point that kept coming to her mind was … if Sarah wanted to be a mother she would have gone looking for her. Surely she would have tried to find her again, and so she stayed silent.

On the day of the funeral, she, Sarah and Glen stood at her mother's gravesite, their arms linked as they listened to the prayers and poems recited, aware of those present mainly being hostel staff. Tears rolled on Sarah's and Aimee's cheeks. As the service ended, Sarah put a protective arm around Aimee's shoulders, and the three walked away together.

Back at Trailblazers, Aimee wandered down to see Thor and Louie, their contact soothing the dull ache in her heart, for a while at least. Soon she would have to pack her things and leave – she had her own house now and shouldn't be a burden on Sarah any longer. She had noted the change in Sarah since Glen had come on the scene and Sarah's life was now changing too –

it would only be a matter of time …

"Penny for your thoughts," she heard Sarah's voice behind her.

She unburied her face from Thor's mane and unsuccessfully fought back her tears. She wiped them away.

"Missing Monnie?"

Aimee nodded and rested her brow back on Thor. "He's a good listener though," she murmured.

Sarah sighed. "Life goes on, hon. It's there to live, and sometimes we just have to live with our decisions and move on." She rubbed Aimee's shoulder gently. "It seems the best things that ever come my way in life I let go of when I shouldn't. You live with the decisions, but the regrets always remain. "

Aimee nodded. She should have stayed with her mother instead of going to Perth. She should have spent more time with her while she could and not been off chasing her dream.

"Your mum was so proud of you, you know. She told me once that this was the life you should always have had, as if you were born to it." Sarah half-smiled. "It was the one thing we really agreed on. Just remember, you are like the daughter I always wished I'd had."

Aimee forced a smile, imagining that conversation. "Well, I guess it's over now," she said. "The dream came true, and now life goes on."

Sarah frowned and her head tilted. "What do you mean?"

"I've inherited the house so I guess it's time to …"

"What?" Sarah's eyes flew open in stunned surprise. "You don't have to leave, sweetie! Not unless you want to." She gazed at her intently. "Do you want to?" She swallowed thickly, her eyes misting over.

Aimee shook her head. It would be like losing her mother all over again.

"Oh, thank god," Sarah gushed. "You've been here so long

you're part of the team … and who's going to fill up that new trophy cabinet Glen has been looking at lately? … and Thor and Louie would be devastated."

Aimee's lips hinted at a smile. "I just thought with you and Glen …."

"That's what I came down to tell you – Glen and I are engaged."

Aimee's smile instantly beamed. Then she noticed Glen standing in the background and gave him a wink.

"Thor and Louie will get you back where you are now, in time, and we will never sell them," Sarah added. "I regret shunning Glen when we first met years ago, but not this time." She smiled warmly. "Now we will move on together, we will all move on together."

"… and your other regret?" Aimee asked.

Sarah sighed. "Standing at the gravesite today, I realised my greatest mistake was giving up my daughter and never trying to find her. I have felt that regret most strongly since you came to stay. I regret that when I die my daughter will have never known me … she will never know who I was. She is my greatest regret and I can never undo that loss."

Aimee's hand covered her mouth to quell her sobs as tears flowed onto her cheeks. All her dreams had now come true. She grabbed Thor's neck to keep herself upright.

"Aimee, what the matter? What's wrong? What …?"

Glen started moving forward, sensing the growing turmoil.

"When I was going through Mum's things," Aimee blurted out, pulling a paper from her inside coat pocket where she kept it close to her heart. "I found adoption papers … my adoption papers! My real name is Marjorie Aimee Brown …" she said, holding up the document.

Sarah's mouth fell open.

"You are listed as my birth mother …"

Sarah squealed and tears poured onto her cheeks. Crying and smiling, she grabbed Aimee, dragged her into her arms and clutched onto her tightly. Glen's arms embraced them both.

"… and life goes on," he said drily. "Looks like I've just gained a ready-made family."

"We need tissues …" Sarah's and Aimee's muffled voices came from within the huddle. "…and chocolate … Lots and lots of chocolate!"

*****

About the Author

Pam is a primary school teacher who was obsessed with horses from a very early age. Born in Western Australia to non-horsey parents she spent most of her spare time playing with the horses. She then went on to do the occasional coaching at various pony clubs.

She is married to the most amazing husband Bruce and has two incredibly talented children none of which are horsey. Sadly, Pam's horsey endeavours came to an abrupt end in 2014 after a serious accident that now prohibits her from riding.

With time on her hands, Pam wrote the book to highlight the benefits of helping people to understand how being dedicated to a sport can enhance your ability to be resilient and independent, and that most problems have a solution. You just have to look for them.